TEMPT ME
Isabel Morin

Chapter One

At some point during her going away party, people Nina had never met began arriving. Which was fine, since she hadn't been in New York long enough to acquire a roomful of friends. Even the people she did know were more Stacy's friends than hers. But it was sweet of Stacy to throw the party just the same.

Nina was standing by the iPod dock in the corner, fooling around with the music, when Stacy walked over, a wicked grin on her face.

"Nina, I have someone I'd like you to meet," she said, turning halfway around to smile at a man who'd followed her across the room. "Ian Sinclair, meet the woman of honor, Nina Valentine."

Stacy winked at Nina and disappeared back into the group of people standing around the drinks table.

Six foot something of gorgeous manliness stood before her in perfectly tailored suit pants, crisp white shirt rolled up to his elbows and unbuttoned at the throat, and a loosened lavender tie at his neck. Early-thirties, dark wavy hair and Paul Newman eyes, not to mention the lean body of an athlete.

Were men like him even allowed into BYOB parties at rundown fifth floor walk-ups in the East Village? She only hoped he wasn't some Wall Street guy. Corporate types left her cold.

"Nice tie," she said, then immediately worried her attempt at sassiness would be taken as sarcasm.

"You think?" he asked, looking down at the article in question. "I wasn't sure about it at first, but in the end I decided to subvert the usual masculine color paradigm."

Nina grinned, already charmed. "I'd say you're pulling it off."

"I appreciate the compliment, especially coming from the guest of honor. I wondered whose party I was crashing. I came with my buddy Phil straight from work," he said, gesturing toward the only other man in the room wearing a button-down shirt and tie.

"Most of these people are Stacy's friends, or people she works with at the restaurant she manages. I haven't been in the city long enough to fill a room, so it's just as well we have crashers," Nina said, laughing ruefully. "Where do you work?"

"At a law firm uptown."

A lawyer. Nina's heart sank. What would she have in common with a lawyer? Then again, what did she need to have in common with him? They were just talking after all.

"Not too impressed with lawyers, huh?" he asked, and Nina wished she weren't so transparent. But he was smiling good-naturedly, so he must not have been too offended.

"Sorry, I guess I've just been around artistic types too long. I'm not sure I've ever spoken to an actual lawyer."

"Well, don't judge us too harshly. Some of us can be pretty good company," he said, winking at her before taking a sip of his beer.

A frisson of heat ran through her at his flirtatious reply. Nervously she started to take a sip of wine, only to discover her glass was empty.

"Can I get you a refill?" he asked.

"That would be great. Something red, please," she said, relieved he'd broken the tension.

Smiling, Ian took her glass and headed across the room to the makeshift bar outside the galley kitchen door. Quickly, darting a look to make sure he wasn't watching, she moved over a few steps to check her reflection in the mirror hanging across the room.

She'd arrived in New York with the same long, slightly wavy hair she'd had for years, but a few weeks ago her hairdresser had sat her in the chair and met her gaze in the mirror.

"I have women who pay hundreds of dollars a year to get your gorgeous sable color, but you need a style. Let me make you look like you belong in Manhattan."

Nina had nervously acquiesced, and when Sharon was finished, Nina had gone from an attractive duck to a swan, or at least a sexier duck. Sharon had given her long layers and bangs that just brushed her eyebrows.

"There," the hairdresser had declared, spinning Nina around in her swivel chair until she faced the mirror. "Now we can see your pretty heart-shaped face. It's the Zooey Deschanel look, and you're at least as pretty as her."

"No need to go overboard, Sharon," Nina had laughed, but she'd loved it.

Feminine yet sophisticated, her new look made her more confident, especially tonight in her black pencil skirt, silvery silk halter top and black knee-high boots with three-inch heels. This was the best she ever looked, so it would have to be good enough for Ian.

Quickly she returned to where they'd been standing and watched as Ian made his way back to her with her wine and a fresh beer for himself. He had an athlete's physical ease with his body, and even in his professional clothes she could see the play of muscles as he moved.

"So when do you leave our fair city?" he asked, handing her the glass.

"On Wednesday. Somehow I have to get everything I own into a rental car. Then it's back to New Hampshire for me."

"What's in New Hampshire?"

Nina couldn't help making a face. "My hometown, my mother. Grim reminders of my high school years. The usual."

"Nina!" Her friend Kelly from the frame shop was suddenly beside her, laughing and hugging her.

"I didn't think you'd make it," Nina said, forcing herself to pay attention to her co-worker, though she remained utterly aware of Ian. He continued to watch her, his gaze dark and intent.

"I had to come," Kelly said, excitable as always. "I was afraid I wouldn't see you before you left. You would not believe the people who've interviewed for your job. I'm going to hate whoever takes your place."

Nina introduced Kelly and Ian, hoping Kelly would leave gracefully. No such luck.

"Carol and Stan are here, too," Kelly added, gesturing toward the bar.

Nina pasted a smile on her face. Obviously she had to go say hi. God willing, she'd be able to pick up again with Ian in just a few minutes.

"Sorry, I'd better go play hostess," she said, smiling apologetically at him. "Don't go anywhere."

"Oh, I won't," he replied, and his smile was enough to make her believe him.

***

Ian watched Nina get dragged away from him and tried to quell his frustration. Taking a long pull on his beer, he contented himself with watching her while he considered whether he'd be able to get her to come home with him. Was it possible to steal a person away from her own going-away party?

She was laughing with a group of people now, her glossy, dark hair occasionally obscuring her face. Then she'd turn toward the guy standing to her left and he'd see her expression, her eyes bright with humor. Every so often she glanced over at him and smiled, as if to say she hadn't forgotten him, so he was pretty sure they'd be able to pick up where they left off, sooner or later. He just had to be patient.

Christ, her body was unbelievable. Curves in all the right places, incredible shoulders. If she wasn't leaving so soon he'd have considered restraining himself tonight and asking her out for dinner, but there wasn't time for the usual dating rituals. Besides, he'd probably explode sitting across from her through an entire meal, pretending he wasn't thinking about getting her naked.

His friend Phil, a junior partner in another law firm, sidled over, beer in hand, and smirked at him.

"You realize you've been standing here for fifteen minutes, watching that woman like you're about to drag her off to your cave?"

"That's exactly what I'm hoping to do," he said, reluctantly shifting his gaze away from Nina.

"Dude," Phil said, with a pointed look, "just relax and try not to look like you're gonna take out every guy that talks to her. You need to try to pass for a civilized human being or you'll scare her off."

"What? I'm not..." he began before trailing off. He let out a long sigh. "Point taken. But in ten more minutes I'm moving in."

"God speed, buddy," Phil said, clinking his bottle to Ian's before draining his own. "Need another?" he asked, his body already turned toward the bar.

"Thanks, I'm good," Ian replied. He needed to stay sharp tonight.

*****

Nina finally broke away and headed back through the crowd, which had gotten crazier as people drank and danced. Ian stood watching her from the back of the room, and her heart beat a mile a minute at the hungry look in his eye. This guy was hers for the taking, if she had the nerve to follow through. She wasn't sure she did yet. He was so much more than she was used to – insanely good looking, confident, outrageously sexy. In other words, out of her league, though the way he was looking at her, he didn't seem to know it.

"Sorry about that," she said when she'd reached him. "I didn't think I'd be gone so long."

"No worries. This is your party after all."

"True, but I think that about does it for the people I know here, so we should be safe."

He smiled at that and his gaze drifted down, taking her in with one thorough, appreciative glance, and suddenly she didn't feel so safe. She felt as if she were on the brink of something deliciously dangerous.

"So, you were saying something about leaving Wednesday in a rented car?"

"Oh, right," she said, relieved he was taking the conversational lead. "Well, everything but my paintings," she said, gesturing at the walls. "I'll come back and get them next time I visit. The ones I haven't given to Stacy, anyway."

Ian looked at the painting nearest to them, then at the others around the room.

"You did these?" he asked, moving closer to the one behind her.

One of her moodier pieces.

"Yes, this is from my mad as hell period," she said, making a sweeping gesture, like a tour guide in a museum. "Note the frantic brush strokes, the bright slashes of red."

He looked at her speculatively. "You don't need to joke about them. I'm no expert, but even I can see these are the real deal."

Nina ducked her head, embarrassed by his straightforward compliment. Her art meant everything to her, but lately she'd begun losing faith in herself. She was only twenty-seven, and already she felt washed up.

"Oh, thanks. I guess I'm a little too quick with the self-deprecation. I'm just a little worn down," she admitted. "Being a starving artist gets old after a while. But I'm not sorry I came. New York always seemed like the ideal place to paint, and I still think that. Maybe my timing was just off."

"Looks like mine is too. Just my luck to meet you right before you leave."

"I'm not gone yet," Nina replied, the words leaving her mouth before she realized what she was saying.

Mortified, knowing her face was blazing, she looked down at her wine with utter concentration. What was wrong with her? She was practically throwing herself at the man and she'd known him less than an hour.

Ian said nothing. When she dared look at him again she saw he'd gone utterly still. His gaze moved from her eyes to her mouth.

"No, you're not gone yet," he repeated, his low voice sending a shiver along her spine. It was the bedroomiest voice she'd ever heard, and the sound of it affected her like a touch. Just like that she was fully aroused, her nipples tightening, her pulse racing.

Slowly he walked toward her, pressing her back against the wall, his hands on her hips as his mouth descended.

Nothing in her life had ever felt so good. He was a slow burn, his tongue slipping between her lips to explore, plunging and stroking with leisurely devastation. Without hesitation she opened for him, oblivious to the party around her as she wrapped her arms around his neck. He shut out all sound, all thought, everything but the feel and taste of him.

His hands left her hips and moved to her waist, then higher, his thumbs stroking just below her breasts as his mouth moved down her throat. She could feel him hard against her and his own arousal stoked hers higher. Finally he pulled away, his breathing ragged as he looked down at her.

"Christ, Nina, let me take you home."

Everything in her wanted to say yes, but she hesitated, so out of her element she didn't know how to reply. He was so overwhelming. Would she be enough for him?

He groaned at her hesitation, his lips on her neck, on her mouth again, urgent and dark.

"Yes, yes, I'll come," she gasped out, a mewl escaping her as he nipped at her lower lip, as if in punishment for hesitating.

"I'll wait while you say your goodbyes," he said, letting his hands caress her bare shoulders before letting her go. "I'm not fit to be seen anyway," he said ruefully, and Nina couldn't help but look down. He was huge and hard, and the thought of him filling her left her lightheaded.

"You keep looking at me like that, we won't make it out the door."

That did it. Shaking her head and swaying the tiniest bit, Nina made her way over to where Stacy stood talking to several women Nina didn't know. As soon as Nina approached, her friend grabbed her arm and pulled her to the side.

"Holy shit. What I wouldn't give to have Ian Sinclair's tongue down my throat. I've known him over a year but he's never looked twice at me."

"Then you won't be mad if I leave now?"

"Consider him your going-away present. Never say I didn't do anything for you."

"I've never gone home with a man I knew less than an hour. A year in this city has turned me into a big ol' slut."

"A smart, happy slut. Have a good time," she said, giving Nina a kiss on the check.

Hurriedly, somehow afraid that if she took too long he'd change his mind, she slipped on a light jacket, grabbed her toothbrush, makeup bag and hairbrush and threw them into her purse.

He was waiting by the door. He had his suit jacket on and was talking to his friend but looking around the room every few seconds. As soon as he saw her he grinned, his eyes lighting up as his gaze raked her from top to bottom with obvious pleasure.

He directed an insanely sexy smile at her as she approached.

"All set?" he asked.

They left the apartment and headed down the five flights, emerging from the stagnant, overheated air of the stairwell to the exhilarating chill of the early October night.

Nina stopped and breathed deeply, her whole body buzzing with energy, as alive and ready as the city itself.

She laughed and turned to Ian, shaking her head.

"I don't even know where you're taking me. Where do you live?"

"Will you change your mind of I tell you I live on the Upper West Side? It sounds so obnoxious, but hell, it's a great neighborhood."

"Are you kidding me? I've never been seduced by someone from the Upper West Side. This is a huge step up for me."

Ian laughed and lifted a hand to hail a cab. The light at First Avenue and Tenth Street turned green and a cab swung to the curb. Ian opened the door for her, but just as she was about to slide in, a horrible thought popped into her head.

This man expected hot sex from her. He probably got the ultimate in sexy New York females whenever he had the itch, which meant he was sure to be disappointed with her small town moves.

Nina turned to Ian, her cheeks burning even before she spoke.

"Listen, I'm not... I don't have a lot of tricks or anything. My outfit probably gave you a certain impression or whatever, but the thing is I'm actually pretty tame."

He looked at her as if he didn't know whether to be amused or irritated.

"Nina," he started, then stopped, shaking his head. "You don't have to come if you're that nervous. But if you do want to come home with me, it'll just be us having a good time. I might be crazed with lust for you, but I'm not some, what do you call it, toxic bachelor. I don't expect elaborate physical feats."

"Oh, okay. Sorry," she said, relieved and embarrassed in equal measure.

The cabbie was less tolerant. "You two coming, or what?" he yelled.

Ian raised his eyebrows in question and she smiled and slid into the car, her heart picking up its pace when he got in beside her. Leaning forward he gave the driver his address.

"How exactly do you know about toxic bachelors?" Nina asked, teasing but very much wanting an answer. "Are you one of those rare men who's a *Sex and the City* fan?"

"Hell, no. But my sister lived with me for a while, and I was subjected to it on a regular basis. She told me I needed to watch it so I'd understand women."

"Did it work?"

"You tell me," he replied, smiling wickedly at her as he leaned back in the seat, looking at her like he was trying to decide where to start licking first.

"So far so good," she replied, wondering to herself if there was such a thing as knowing women *too* well.

She heard something vibrating and was about to look in her purse when he pressed a hand to his suit pocket. "It's mine," he said, taking his cell phone out and looking at the number with a frown. "Damn, I have to take this. I'll just be a second."

"What's up, Scott?" he said, all business. There was a pause as he listened, a frown of concentration or displeasure on his face. He looked different in some subtle way. Intense, a bit harder. "I was afraid that was going to happen. Go back to them and tell them no way. The union was very clear about how much they'd give up." Another pause. "No, I'll let you take care of this one," he said, glancing over at Nina. "Yes, really. Just stick to the script. They have a show to put on. They'll give in."

He hung up and shoved his phone back in his pocket.

"Everything all right?" Nina asked, curious but reluctant to pry.

"Yeah, it's fine. My law firm is handling the stagehand union's demands for better benefits. The producers of a couple of shows threw down this evening and one of my guys wanted to check in about how to proceed."

"One of your guys? So you're, like, the boss of the negotiations?" Nina asked.

"I'm a partner in the firm and I specialize in entertainment and sports law, so I'm lead counsel on this one. But there's no need for me to get involved tonight. Scott can handle it." He paused a moment. "I hope."

"If you have to go..." Nina began, seriously hoping he wouldn't take her up on the offer. She hadn't realized he was so successful, and the idea sent a new thrill through her. It was primitive and ridiculous, but there it was.

"I'm not going anywhere," he said. "Unless you changed your mind about coming over," he said, looking worried.

"No, I still want to come."

"Thank God for that," he said. He leaned forward in his seat and peered out the windshield. "Are we there yet?"

The taxi made its slow way uptown. Nina had wondered if Ian would put any moves on her in the cab, but instead he took her hand in his big warm grip and held on, his thumb idly stroking her palm.

It was only ten o'clock, early for Manhattan, and there were people everywhere on such a beautiful night. She and Ian traded comments on the sights they passed, acting like mature adults, but all the while she was so conscious of his every move, she didn't know how she kept drawing breath. He seemed even bigger in the confines of the car, and everywhere they touched or almost touched her body flared with awareness. Desperate for some kind of distraction before she spontaneously combusted, she asked him the question she'd been dying to know.

"This is going to sound really juvenile, but do you represent any famous people?"

He grinned, not at all surprised by the question.

"Well, yeah, but it's not as exciting as it sounds. I hardly ever meet the clients. Usually I'm talking to their agent or another attorney. But I can get front row seats to just about any event in town, so if you're ever back and want to see a Broadway show or go to a Knicks game..."

Nina didn't know what to say to this. Did he really think she'd call him for such a thing?

"I have met Barry Manilow," he said, leaning in and whispering in her ear, as if he were telling her something confidential.

"I love him," she exclaimed, unable to contain her glee. "When I was a kid I found a tee shirt with a Barry Manilow Iron-On at a tag sale and I wore it every day for weeks."

"Now that is hot," he laughed.

They were in his neck of the woods now, in a neighborhood utterly different from the areas she'd grown familiar with during her short stay in the city. It was way cleaner for one thing, and the streets were lined with boutiques and restaurants. Lots of sushi and upscale Italian, and a store that sold only hats, the wide-brimmed, flower-bedecked kind rich women wore to horse races and garden parties. Gorgeous, but how did anyone wear them without feeling ridiculous?

At last the taxi pulled up to the curb in front of a row of brownstones. Ian handed the driver a twenty and told him to keep the change before getting out. Nina slid over the seat, surprised to find him waiting to help her out of the car. She'd obviously been dating the wrong sort of men, because no one had ever done such a simple thing. It pleased her enormously and went a long way toward making her feel like less of a harlot. Or if she was a harlot, she was a high class one.

Even better, he held onto her hand as they entered his building. The foyer was marble and had a certain Edith Wharton feel – elegant and austere.

It was easier to concentrate on the architecture, since she could barely look at Ian.

"Nice place," she commented inanely. God, she sounded like such a rube. She needed to get a grip.

"Yeah, I was lucky to get it. These co-ops are crazy. They do everything short of a cavity search before they let you in."

They rode the elevator in silence, Nina keeping her eye on the numbers as they lit up. There were ten floors, and they went straight to the top.

She was always nervous before having sex for the first time. Her friends liked to kid her for being such a delicate flower. But the hot kiss and the cab ride over had stoked her to the point of wanting to jump him. The man's body was like nothing she'd ever seen outside of magazines and J. Crew catalogs.

The elevator opened onto a hall with a heavy gold mirror hanging opposite them, and she blinked at the sight of herself next to him. They looked good together, like they belonged.

He led her past two enormous doors that looked like they'd been salvaged from a medieval castle before stopping at number 1004. He gave her a smile that was somehow suggestive and reassuring at the same time as he unlocked the door, allowing her to enter first.

It was too dark to make out much of anything, though light from outside filtered through windows in the distance. One thing was obvious – his place was a hell of a lot bigger than hers.

She watched as he closed the door and flicked on a light switch, illuminating them in the warm glow of a stained-glass standing lamp. Yup, he still looked good enough to eat.

Without a word he came toward her, his hands on her hips as he bent down and took her mouth. He was slow and thorough, and for the first time she knew what it was to be kissed by a man rather than a guy. Even as she felt the tension rise and coil between them, he took his time, his slow, drugging kisses drawing her out rather than rushing her.

"You are so gorgeous," he murmured into her ear as his mouth brushed along her jaw and down her throat.

Her mouth opened under his, letting him in, holding nothing back. God, he tasted good, the dark notes of beer and need pulling her under. One hand slid beneath the silk hem of her shirt while the other cupped her ass, bringing her into full contact with his arousal.

He used his entire body, pressing into her until she felt him in every pore, her skin humming with the feel of him. His big hands burrowed into her hair as he kissed her senseless.

Then his heat left her as he pulled away. She opened her eyes, dazed and bereft. "What? Why did you stop?"

"Maybe I ought to cool my jets," he said, shoving his hands in his pockets, as if to keep them safely away from her. "I don't want to get carried away too quick and scare you off."

"But I liked it."

"Yeah, me too," he said, laughing shakily. "Jesus, Nina. You're so goddamn sexy," he said, and then he kissed her again, long and slow and achingly hot. "Even your skin..."

He tried to pull away again but she wouldn't let him. "You don't need to worry about me, Ian. I'm right there with you."

For an instant he remained frozen, looking at her with something like awe or fascination, and then he came back to her. This time he wasn't holding back. All the heat in him, the power of his fine-tuned athlete's body was bent on her, focused on the two of them coming together.

His mouth came down to hers, hungry and demanding. She met him with demands of her own now, pushing his jacket off him, all self-consciousness evaporating in her need to feel more of him. Ian took her cue, pulling his tie off and throwing it on the floor as if tossing aside the last vestiges of his polished, civilized self. Nina lifted her silk blouse over her head and let it drift to the floor beside his tie before going to work on his shirt. Soon it, too, was at their feet.

Beautiful. He was just what a man should be. Not pumped up out of vanity, but hard with useful muscle.

"Jackpot," she breathed. She ran her hands over him, letting her fingers graze his nipples before pulling him closer. "Whatever you do to look like this, let me tell you, it's worth it."

He murmured something against her neck.

"What was that?" she asked, her voice high and breathless from his hands and mouth.

He smoothed his hands over her curves, down over her hips until he reached the bottom of her skirt.

"Triathlons," he repeated distractedly, all the while kissing his way down her throat as his hands moved up her thighs.

Images of his gorgeous body being put through its paces flashed through her brain. That was it. She needed him on top of her. Now.

"Show me your bedroom, Ian."

Chapter Two

His eyes blazed and he grabbed her hand, pulling her through an enormous, high-ceilinged living room, past an office and into his bedroom. Vaguely she noticed it was a fantastic apartment, but all she could focus on was Ian.

When they reached the bedroom he turned and kissed her, his hands rough with urgency as they brushed over her shoulders and down her arms, coming to rest at her hips. His lips opened over hers, his tongue stroking into her mouth. Slow, deep kisses that stole her breath and left her wanting still more.

She ached for him, out of her mind with the need to be filled by his heat. His erection pressed hot and hard against her belly and she ran her hand between their bodies, cupping him, reveling in his size and desire.

A harsh moan escaped him at her touch. A flush darkened his cheekbones and his eyes were wild. Without a word Nina moved to the side of his bed and sat down. Her eyes on his, feeling sexier than she ever had in her life, she unzipped her boots, her long hair brushing her overly sensitized skin as she moved.

She let her skirt ride up, showing the edge of her thigh-high black stockings.

"You're killing me, Nina," he said, falling to his knees between her thighs. His hands stroked her from ankle to the lacey edge of her stockings, thumbs rubbing the skin just beyond.

Nina's head fell back, pushing her breasts in their black lace bra forward. Ian's mouth was on her, peeling away the lace cup to suck and bite her nipples, one and then the other as his hand found and cupped her pussy through the thin silk of her black underwear.

Nina ran her hands over him, glorying in the way his muscles flexed with each move he made. Her hands raked over his back as she pressed her mouth to his throat, tasting heat and salt. Slowly, wanting to drive him crazy, she unclasped his belt and unbuttoned him. Her hand paused teasingly over the zipper until his hand grabbed her wrist, either to stop her or make her go on.

Slanting a look up at him through her lashes, she looked at where his lean stomach and the chiseled edges of his hip bones disappeared into his pants. She needed to feel him, needed him inside her as soon as possible. His breathing was hoarse as she released his zipper and pulled his boxers down, freeing his cock.

He was huge and hot, the length of him throbbing for her. She stroked him once, twice, and was rewarded by a long moan before he abruptly pulled away and shed the rest of his clothes.

He was perfectly formed, beautifully muscled and rigid with desire. With one move he had her skirt and underwear off, though she still wore her stockings.

"Hurry," she said, spreading her thighs for him, so far gone with need she touched herself for relief.

She heard his quick intake of breath before he pulled her hand away. His eyes were on hers, watching her every reaction as he sucked her finger. She felt the pull deep down, an ache that was growing by the second.

"You taste so good, baby. I need more of it," he said, kneeling before her again and spreading her open.

"Oh God, yes," she breathed at the first touch of his tongue. He lapped her up in long, slow strokes that had her hips rising off the bed and her thighs trembling. Her fingers tangled in his hair, urging him on, keeping him there. In answer he thrust his tongue inside of her.

She cried out, desperate now for him, and moved back until she was fully on the bed. He rose above her, his face tight with restraint as he leaned over her to open the drawer of his nightstand. Kneeling between her legs he ripped open the condom packet, his hands shaking, and sheathed himself in seconds flat.

His eyes locked on hers and she gripped his ass, urging him on.

"Now, Ian. Please," she whimpered, well beyond caring that she was begging for him.

He entered her slowly, filling her so exquisitely her back arched off the bed and she wrapped her legs around him. With each thrust he took her higher, his cock hitting her sweet spot until she was nearly sobbing with pleasure.

Her legs rose straight into the air, wanting him deeper and deeper still. Then she touched herself, stroking her clit to his rhythm while he watched himself go in and out, watched her fingers.

Pleasure built to a nearly unendurable peak and then broke over her, her body pulsing with sensation, pushed further by Ian driving into her with abandon, his hands fisted in her hair, his eyes on hers. He drove her half a foot up the bed as he came apart saying her name.

Spasms still wracked him as he collapsed on top of her, somehow not crushing her with his weight. He felt wonderful, and she wrapped her arms around him, glorying in his powerful body.

He raised his head and kissed her, a sloppy, relaxed, utterly sexy kiss she felt all the way down to her toes. Then carefully withdrawing he pulled off the condom, expertly tying a knot in the end, and tossed it toward the trash basket across the room.

"Nice shot," she said as it went in.

"Is that all you have to say, Miss Nina?" he said, rolling her toward him until she lay on his chest.

Laughing and completely energized, she sat up and gave him a long look, drinking him in.

"Fishing for compliments?" she asked, running her hand over his thigh and six-pack abs and up to his chest. "I think you know you rocked my world, but I don't mind saying it. That was hands down the best sex I've ever had."

He started to say something but she cut him off. "You totally don't have to say it was your best sex. I feel way too fantastic to even care if you liked it," she teased.

"I hate to spoil things for you then, but that was the best sex I've had, bar none. But I think we might be able to do even better if we practice."

Leaning over she kissed him once more for good measure, then swung her legs over the side of the bed and stood up. "I have to pee," she explained over her shoulder, knowing he watched her as she left the room and loving it.

She did her business and then washed her hands, examining her face in the mirror. Pretty much the same as always, but better. Her dark hair was messy, but in a good, I-just-got-laid kind of way, and her skin was flushed and, well, glowing. Her lips were fuller too, and she couldn't help pouting like a model in a magazine.

Feeling guilty but too curious to stop herself, she looked through his linen closet and medicine cabinet. Nothing too crazy in either one. Tiger balm and wraps for sprains, pain killers. A box of condoms, extra large.

No kidding.

She sagged against the wall for just a second as she recalled him filling her, and then she shook herself and headed back for the real thing.

Halfway down the hall her heart gave a little thump.

What exactly happened now?

It was late, so she assumed she'd be sleeping over, but what if that wasn't what he had in mind?

She stopped in the doorway, awkward and shy and wondering what she should say, her light-hearted confidence evaporating.

Ian had moved. Now rather than lying diagonally across the bed looking half-dead, he'd gotten under the covers and lay with his head on a pillow. He sat up on an elbow and smiled at her.

"Hey gorgeous, get over here. The troops are getting restless."

And just like that her worries drained away. She walked to the bed, smiling as she stripped off her stockings and slipped under the covers.

He wrapped an arm around her waist and pulled her back into the curve of his body until they were spooning like they'd been lovers for years.

"I'm spent, woman," he said into her hair. "You'll have to wait at least a couple of minutes before I'm worth anything."

She was exhausted, but alert too, alive to every breath he took, his scent, the feel of him pressed against her. A slight melancholy came over her at the thought that she'd be gone soon, and who knew if she'd even see him after tomorrow?

She wouldn't sleep of course. It took her ages to be able to sleep well with a new guy, but that was okay. This way she'd enjoy the feel of him all night long.

It was the last thought she had before she fell asleep.

When she woke up it was early morning, the sun just risen. She stretched lazily and then got up to use the bathroom, padding silently through his palatial apartment, peeking into rooms as she went. When she got back to bed Ian was awake and smiling drowsily at her.

"Hey there," he said, pulling back the covers for her. "Come back in and get warm."

She lay in his arms, relaxing against his deliciously warm body as she gazed at the pen and ink sketches of the city hanging on the opposite wall.

"Does my art pass muster?" he asked, nuzzling her neck. "I saw those in a gallery I was passing by and thought they were interesting."

"As a matter of fact, it does," she said. "You have a good eye."

"I'd rather have your work on the wall. Maybe I could buy something of yours."

"The hell you will," she said, looking at him with censure. "I'll give you a piece if you really want one, but there's no way I'm taking your money."

"Okay, okay. I just think you should get paid for your work, that's all. Did you ever try to get your paintings into a gallery here?"

"Sure. I tried a bunch of galleries, and I've placed in a few good juried shows. Even won a couple," she said, glad she could tell him that. "There's a gallery in Chelsea that liked the direction I was going in and told me to bring my new work by."

"Wow. So what happened? Did they take anything?"

Now Nina was wishing she hadn't brought any of this up. She could feel her face flame before she even spoke.

"Well, I wasn't able to finish enough paintings."

"What do you mean?" he said, sitting up and frowning at her. "Chances like that don't come along every day. You can't waste an invitation like that, no matter how talented you are."

She sat up, pulling the covers to her chest. How dare he talk to her like that? He had no idea what she'd gone through trying to scrape together enough money to paint. Moving to New York had been both the best and worst decision she could have made for her work. She got seen, and then she couldn't afford to stay to see it all through. The thought of it just about broke her heart.

"It's not like I just blew it off. Do you have any idea how expensive paints are, not to mention brushes, canvas, framing? It was all I could do to pay my rent. I ran out of supplies a few months ago and didn't have the money to replace them. That's why I'm leaving. There's no point staying here if I can't even paint."

There was a long silence while Nina stared down at the blue quilt on the bed, pinching the material between her fingers.

"I'm sorry," he said, lying back down and taking her with him. "I didn't realize things were so rough for you. Forgive me?"

He felt so good, it was impossible to stay mad at him, especially after his simple and sincere apology.

"Of course I forgive you. But I don't want you feeling sorry for me. It's not like I'm a poor orphan child or anything. My childhood was perfectly comfortable. It's just that my parents didn't want me studying art. I wasn't even supposed to apply to art schools, but I did it anyway. I got into The Art Institute of Chicago, but even that didn't change their minds."

"You mean they didn't give in?"

Nina laughed. "My parents don't give in to anything. They wanted me to study science or business, something practical. If I had they'd have paid for everything. They told me if I studied art it would be without any help from them. And it was."

She fell silent then, reluctant to talk about those years. She'd had to work too many hours just to pay for a ratty apartment in a sketchy neighborhood. More than anything she'd wanted the time to soak up and enjoy the possibilities opening up for her, but instead she was constantly worried, always tired, and never quite sure she could afford to come back the next semester. Worse, she had never quite forgiven her parents for not understanding her.

Ian rolled on top of her and her legs opened naturally for him to settle in.

"I like a woman with conviction," he murmured, bending down to kiss her.

The kiss turned deeper, their bodies moving together with a new sense of ease even as they discovered one another all over again. Instead of the urgent sex of last night, it was slow and intense, sleepy and languorous. His roughened jaw against her neck and sensitized breasts set her aflame, and she twined her arms and legs around his big, gorgeous body and rode the wave until it took her under again.

The second time she woke up, Ian was asleep beside her and the sun was peeking around his curtains. She leaned over to check the clock on his bedside table.

Shit. It was nearly nine o'clock.

Panicked, she got up quietly, not wanting to waken Ian just yet, and dragged her clothes on. What she had of them, anyway. Her shirt was somewhere by the door.

"What are you doing?"

Nina jumped guiltily at the sound of Ian's voice, still blurred with sleep.

"I'm so sorry. I didn't meant to sleep so late and then have to run, but today's my last day at the frame shop. I'm due in at eleven and I still need to get all the way downtown, shower and change and then get across town to the West Village."

Ian sat up, the blanket falling away from his bare chest. He looked sleepy and confused, totally adorable. It was all she could do not to climb back into bed.

He scrubbed his face with his hands and then swung his legs over the side of the bed and stood up, the sight of him so overpowering it was almost a relief when he pulled on a pair of blue track pants and a faded gray tee shirt.

"At least let me call you a car. You can have a cup of coffee while you wait."

Call her a car? Who did that?

"Um. That's not necessary. I can take the subway," she said.

"If I call now it'll be here in fifteen minutes. You can use it to get home and then to work."

Nina looked at his stubbornly set jaw and saw the glimmer of the lawyer he was by day. He looked pretty determined, so what the hell. It really would make things easier.

"Okay. Call the car. And I'd love some coffee," she said, then headed to the front door for her blouse. Pulling the silk over her head, she couldn't help wishing she had something a little more substantial, a little less walk-of-shame, to wear while she waited.

When she got back to the kitchen Ian was just getting off the phone. As soon as the coffee was ready he poured them each a cup, setting a blueberry muffin in front of her before sitting down himself. It felt oddly intimate, which was ridiculous after the things they'd done to one another in bed.

They made stilted, self-conscious conversation for a little while, and before she knew it the doorman called up to say her ride was downstairs.

Ian walked her to the door and the two of them stood there, at a loss as to what to say. Nina smiled, trying to appear bright and cheerful though she felt suddenly bereft.

"Hang on. I don't even have your number. Let me put it in my phone," he said, heading toward the kitchen. He came back a few seconds later holding his cell phone. "Okay, shoot."

Maybe it was just for show, but even if it was, it was a nice gesture. Ian entered her number as she gave it to him, then smiled at her. He drew her into his arms and kissed her on each cheek, then softly on the mouth.

"I guess you ought to be going," he said, looking at her intently. Then he picked her jacket off the chair and helped her into it.

She opened the door. "Bye, Ian. I had a lovely time."

"Take care of yourself, Nina."

***

All the way home, sitting in the plush back seat of the car, she relived her night with him, everything about it like some urban fantasy but for the vague sense of loss that had settled over her. All day at work she was distracted, the feel of his hands and hot mouth still with her. But if hot memories were all she'd have, then she was going to make the most of them.

She worked her last six hours at the frame shop and returned home, worn out from her eventful night and the sugar crash from her going-away cake. She had just thrown herself onto the couch when her phone rang. It was an unknown number, but she picked it up anyway.

"Nina. It's Ian."

Her heart did something suspiciously close to a leap at the sound of his voice. She sat up and tried to breathe, suddenly not the least bit tired.

"Oh, hi. I didn't expect to hear from you," she said, mentally kicking herself for such a lame reply.

"Listen, I can't stop thinking about you. If you don't have other plans, let me take you out tonight. Anywhere you like."

"Anywhere? Like, I could choose the most expensive restaurant in the city?"

"The sky's the limit," he said, laughter in his voice.

"You pick. There's no food I don't like. I especially love sushi."

"Okay, I'll pick you up at eight, if that's good for you."

Nina hung up the phone, her body already humming at the thought of seeing Ian in – she checked her watch – two hours. What should she wear? She looked around the room, her clothes strewn everywhere, shoes spilling out of the closet. A black garbage bag half-filled with clothes destined for Goodwill sat lopsidedly beside her futon.

Would she be able to find anything in the mess that was her room? And how had she managed to collect so much stuff while living just above the poverty level?

A sound from behind made her jump. Stacy, a smile on her face, watched her from the door.

"Somebody's got a hot date tonight with Mr. Big."

Nina tried and failed to look blasé. "He said he can't stop thinking about me. Not only that, he's coming here to pick me up. Nobody in this city does that."

Stacy's mouth fell open and she clutched her heart. "That is so amazing. I feel like I'm in a movie on the Oxygen network."

"Exactly. This man is clearly out of my league. It's kind of freaking me out."

"Don't be ridiculous," Stacy said dismissively, coming into her room and plopping down on her bed. "I mean, I can see why you might feel that way, him being so handsome and wealthy and nearly perfect from what I can tell –"

"This is so not helping," Nina cut in.

"But he's still just a guy. Anyway the stakes are pretty low, seeing as how you're leaving in four days."

"Exactly, so why is he bothering to see me? I don't get it."

"Nina, you're gorgeous and smart and interesting, and apparently stellar in bed. There's no mystery here."

"If you saw his place you'd know what I mean. The man called me a car, for God's sake. I rode home from my tryst in a black town car."

Stacy sighed. "Never mind. Your lack of awareness is part of your charm, no doubt. What are you going to wear?"

By seven fifty-five, and after a dozen wardrobe changes, she settled on a sage green v-neck sweater that hinted at cleavage without making a big thing of it, a brown corduroy skirt and last night's boots. Some subtle make-up and she was ready to go when Ian buzzed from downstairs.

"Wait there. I'll come down," she yelled into the intercom, since she saw no reason for him to walk up five flights of stairs.

"No way. Let me in, Nina. I'm coming up."

Stacy was getting ready to go to work, but she took time to fake a swoon at this. Nina found it pretty awesome too, but then again, what were five flights to a man who ran triathlons?

Nina opened the door for him, already smiling, only to be struck speechless at the sight of Ian standing before her holding a bouquet of gerbera daisies and baby's breath. Her mouth fell open and her heart beat like mad at the romantic gesture.

How many men would have bought flowers for a woman they'd likely never see again?

Luckily Ian was too busy admiring her to notice her reaction. "You look amazing."

Finally she remembered herself and stepped back, letting him in.

"I can't believe you did this," she said, taking the flowers from him. "Let me find a vase for them."

"I apologize if this was an impractical thing to do, with you leaving so soon."

"Are you kidding? First of all, flowers aren't meant to be practical. Second of all, you don't ever have to apologize for getting a woman flowers."

The car he'd taken was idling at the curb when they got outside. Ian opened the door and let her get in before climbing in himself, grinning like a schoolboy as the car pulled into traffic and made its way uptown to Columbus Circle. Nina stared in shock when they stopped in front of Masa, a five star sushi restaurant with a prix fixe menu that started at over four hundred dollars a person. The fish was flown directly from Japan, for God's sake. Talk about a carbon footprint.

"This is too much," she protested, freaked out at the idea of him spending so much money on her. "You can't take me here. Pick something else."

"I was afraid of this," he said, looking at her with bemusement. "But you did say you love sushi, and it would mean a lot to me to treat you to a fantastic meal, especially with you leaving town. Besides, lawyers make obscene amounts of money. You should think of it as a public service to help me spend some of it."

"So I'd be the Robin Hood of sushi, is that it?"

"Yes, though I guess in this scenario you're Robin Hood and the peasants all rolled into one."

"So I'm a peasant now, huh?" she teased, laughing when he colored a bit.

"Come on, Nina. Give a guy a break. I've never been here before. I wanted to save it for a special occasion and you're it. If it makes you feel any better, I'll make a donation equal to the amount I spend tonight to the organization of your choice."

The thought of eating at such an exclusive restaurant was both frightening and seductive, but the seductive part was winning out. The man sure could talk. No wonder he made so much money. Anyway, when else would she eat such a meal, and with such a man?

"Okay," she said, feeling as if she'd just agreed to something extraordinarily brave, like jumping out of a plane.

He let out a sigh of relief and smiled at her, holding out his hand.

"Let's go eat, baby."

***

"So how was your last day at the frame shop?" he asked. "Were you glad to leave?"

They'd already made their way through five appetizers and were working on the entrée. Everything was spectacular, the fish so fresh it practically melted in her mouth.

She kept her voice low, the way you would in a place of worship. Which is what Masa felt like with its temple-like décor and ambiance.

"I'll miss the people I worked with, and the owner was a sweetie, but I wouldn't complain if I never framed another piece of bad art. I shouldn't complain at all really. It was a decent job, and anyway, I only worked there three days a week. My other income came from painting portraits."

"Portraits, huh? Was that just to pay the bills, or do you like it?" he asked.

"Mostly to pay the bills, though you do learn a lot from it. But I'm not a big fan of painting children, especially babies, and I got a lot of that. It takes ages because they move around so much, and they don't have interesting faces yet. But those weren't the worst. I actually painted a lot of pets."

Ian went into a coughing fit as his sake went down the wrong way. "Pets?" he gasped between coughs. "Say it isn't so."

"Oh, it was so. Sometimes they let me paint Fifi from a photo, but most of the time they wanted it done in person. I guess they thought it was more authentic."

"Jesus, no wonder you're leaving New York."

"It wasn't exactly what I'd imagined for myself when I was in school, but it wasn't all bad. I had some interesting sittings with adults. As humbling as it was, I suppose it's a good reality check for an artist to learn to be less precious about their work. I mean, painters have always painted portraits of rich folks to pay the bills. You're lucky if you get that kind of work. I got a lot of my customers through the frame shop, so it was a pretty good setup."

"Then what went wrong? Why are you leaving?" he asked, looking puzzled.

Nina sighed, looking down at her plate as she made a project out of mixing more wasabi into her soy sauce.

"It would have been great, except I have crazy student loan debt and I could never seem to earn enough to make it all work. I've been worried about money since I graduated high school, and I'm tired. I'm not sure suffering for my art is working for me anymore."

Her stomach clenched thinking about it, and shame washed over her, even though she'd done nothing wrong. But it was one thing to commiserate with people like her who were trying to get by, and another thing to tell a man who thought nothing of paying four hundred dollars for a meal.

She'd been talking at her wine for a few minutes, too embarrassed to look him in the eye as she regaled him with all her failures. Student loan debt and exhaustion probably made her sexy quotient drop pretty dramatically. Then again, why should she care? It wasn't like they were looking to combine bank accounts.

When she finally looked up she saw him watching her speculatively.

"Sounds to me like you worked your ass off and made a lot of sacrifices for what you cared about. Not many people are so committed. Who could blame you for needing to take a break? You'll keep painting when you go back home, right?"

"Yes, I'll always paint," she said with a sigh. At the moment the thought of it weighed on her like a burden. She'd come to the city full of hope about what she'd accomplish, and now she felt like a failure.

"You don't look like you're having very happy thoughts," he said, his voice bringing her out of her head.

"I guess I'm not, but one bite of this food will cure that," she said, determined not to let her woes ruin such an incredible night.

They chatted easily through the rest of the meal, and though she tensed when the check came, she didn't say a word. Ian smiled at her as if he understood her discomfort and gave her hand a squeeze.

"Will you come back to my place, Nina?" he asked, his blue gaze intent on her.

"Hell, yes," she answered, more than ready after sitting across from him for the better part of two hours. Why be coy when there was so little time? "I'd ask you back to my apartment, but it's a mess, what with packing and all."

Ian smiled, obviously pleased by her frank desire. Leaning forward he kissed the back of her hand. Nina started in surprise as a shiver went through her. Her whole body was thrumming in anticipation, only this time without any of the nerves, just the delicious knowledge of how good it was going to be.

They didn't stop touching in the car, and his kiss in the elevator left her stunned and nearly delirious with desire. As soon as they were inside they headed for his bedroom, laughing and breathless.

Together they fell on the bed, pulling at their clothes until they were just skin against skin. Before long Nina was on top, enjoying the view as she straddled him.

"I'm at your mercy," he said, smiling slyly at her.

His hair was mussed and crazy sexy, and he looked good enough to eat.

Leaning over she bit him on the shoulder.

"Whoa," he yelled, laughing and rolling until he was on top of her. He grabbed her hands and held them on either side of her head. "We've got a live one," he whispered, his voice a dark friction that sent shivers down her spine. She watched as his gaze roamed over her face and down her neck to her breasts, entirely open to him as he held her still.

She arched against him in invitation, wanting him inside her. His breathing was ragged, his body tense with need, and still he took his time, moving sinuously over her, letting his cock rub against her clit and groaning at how wet she was.

Only when she was writhing beneath him, her hands in a death grip on his shoulders, did he give her what she needed, entering her with one sure stroke that left her gasping. Deep and slow and steady he set the pace, keeping to it even when she bucked beneath him, desperate to come.

"Not yet, baby," he whispered.

A few more thrusts and he turned her over until she was lying flat on her belly. His hands moved possessively over her, delicately skirting the crease of her ass, then lightly exploring her pussy before one deft finger settled over her clit, stroking her higher.

At last a muscular thigh wedged her legs open and he took her, his body over hers, his weight on his forearms as his hard length filled her. Now it was just sensations. No thought, only need as he wound her tighter and tighter. She was crying out now, thrusting her ass in the air for him, wanting him deeper. Her hands fisted in the sheets as she came, and Ian's hands covered her own, his body moving with hers as he cried out with his own release.

Chapter Three

Ian woke up with his arm wrapped possessively around Nina's waist, her body tucked into his. It was nearly nine, way later than he ever slept. Most Sundays he was up by seven to train, but the last two days he'd completely blown that off. Then again, he was getting a pretty good workout right here in bed.

Carefully, so as not to wake her, he slid out from under the covers. She shifted a bit but continued sleeping, her dark, silky hair spread out on the pillow, a few strands across her cheek. He watched her, still turned on by her long, dark lashes and silky skin, her gorgeous mouth.

Much as he wanted to fool around, she deserved at least a few hours of sleep. Pulling on a pair of jeans and a long-sleeved shirt, he headed into the kitchen to make coffee.

He hummed as he moved around the kitchen, wondering what he should make her for breakfast. Pancakes? An omelet? He'd wait until she was up and let her decide. Or maybe he should run out to the store and get a few things to fancy it up. Fresh strawberries, maybe?

It looked like it was going to be another beautiful day. If she wasn't in a rush to be off, they could walk to the park or even do something touristy like go to the top of the Empire State Building. He hadn't done that in years.

Then he picked up the cell phone he'd left on the table and turned it on. He had a bunch of missed calls and several voicemails. As soon as he listened to the first message he forgot the day he'd been imagining for himself and Nina. The first three messages were from Scott and had been left last night. Each message was increasingly more frantic over the state of the union negotiations. The last call was from one of the senior partners.

"Ian, it's Boyd. Where the hell are you? Things are going down the shitter and no one can get a hold of you. I thought we had this deal locked. Unless you're in a coma you have some explaining to do."

Fuck. What the hell had he been doing mooning around, ignoring his calls? He was a partner for God's sake, a position he'd worked his ass off to get to. He should have known better than to leave everything to Scott. And all this for a woman who was leaving in three days. He must have lost his mind.

Furious with himself, he started making phone calls. Time for some serious damage control.

***

When Nina woke up she was alone. The low murmur of the radio and the scent of coffee floated into the bedroom, pulling her out of her drowsy stupor. Looking at the clock on his nightstand she saw that it was only just after ten o'clock, so she hadn't seriously overstayed her welcome. But she couldn't lie in bed forever, either.

Hoping he wouldn't mind, she grabbed the navy blue terry robe that hung on the back of his door and put it on. She peeked her head out the door to make sure the coast was clear and made for the bathroom.

Quickly she peed, washed her face, brushed her teeth and smoothed her hair until it was not quite a rat's nest. Then she headed for the kitchen.

Ian was on the phone, pacing back and forth across the tiled floor. His hair was still damp from the shower and he was dressed in a suit. His watch glinted on his wrist.

He glanced up at her as she came in but continued talking. His eyes were hard, his jaw tense.

"I said I'd be there. Just give me half an hour, okay? I have some things to tie up."

This definitely wasn't the cozy scene she'd been expecting. Unsure now, she hesitated in the arched doorway and pulled the robe tighter.

He hung up and put the phone in his suit pocket.

"Good, you're up," he said briskly, as if she were a business associate who'd just shown up for a meeting. "Did you want some coffee? I'm afraid I can't offer anything more than that. Something's come up and I have to get going."

"I'm sorry. I didn't mean to sleep so late…"

"Look, it's my fault," he said, his voice terse and impatient. "I took my eye off the ball and now I have some fires to put out. I had no business spending so much time with you. I don't know what I was thinking."

He was frowning at her like there'd been no connection at all between them, no laughing or opening up or unbelievable, mind-blowing sex. Where was the relaxed, sexy man she went home with last night? How could he have turned into this guy?

Nina's gut clenched and she went cold all over, humiliated to be standing in his robe while he looked at her like an inconvenience.

"I'm really sorry you wasted your valuable time on me," she said, hurt causing her voice to shake. "I'll just get out of your hair now." Turning around, she headed for the bedroom, her entire body trembling in reaction.

Ian followed her and stood scowling in the doorway. "There's no need to get all pouty. We both had a good time, but today's a new day."

"That's right, I did have a good time. Too bad you just ruined it," she said, turning her back on him.

She couldn't believe what was happening. All she wanted now was to get away from him before she lost it.

Her silky underwear lay crumpled on the floor like a forgotten party favor. Quickly she pulled it on along with her skirt, letting the robe fall in order to get her bra and sweater on. Ian was still in the doorway but she ignored him as she sat on the bed and pulled on her stockings and boots. No doubt he got a good long look at her legs in the process.

"Nina…"

He took a couple of steps toward her.

Without a word she grabbed her purse and strode past him and out to the front door where she grabbed her coat. She could feel tears threatening and she bit her lip to keep her mouth from turning down the way it did when she was about to cry.

She should have known better than to let down her guard with a guy like him. He was too good-looking, too sure of himself, and way too comfortable kicking her out of his apartment when he was done with her.

All she wanted was to get out of there and get into bed where she could cry in peace. Then she'd tell Stacy all about it and together they'd be outraged and curse men.

But it was a long way between here and there.

They were standing in front of his oversized door in his spacious front hall, but Nina was suddenly claustrophobic. She had to get out of there. Her hand was on the knob when his closed over hers. She could feel the heat of his powerful body near her, sensed his gaze on her face but couldn't bring herself to look at him.

"Let me call you a car," he said, his gruff voice only inches away.

"I can get myself a cab," she said fumbling with the lock now.

"Wait, at least take this," he said, and before she had time to wonder what he was talking about he was shoving money at her. Looking down she saw it was a fifty-dollar bill.

"You can keep your damn money, Ian. That's the last thing I want from you."

She heard his sharp intake of breath and then his hand fell away. She opened the door and walked through it without looking back.

***

Ian stood where he was, barely breathing.

What the hell had he just done?

He walked into his bedroom and stood staring at the twisted sheets, the robe she'd looked so adorable in. He'd just had the most amazing weekend of his life with a woman who was gorgeous, smart, sexy and funny and he'd treated her like shit. Christ, what was wrong with him?

He didn't have time to think about it right now. There'd be plenty of time to examine what a prick he was after he cleaned up the other mess he'd made.

He spent all morning and into the afternoon in negotiations, and it took all his willpower not to dwell on what had happened that morning. All day his stomach was tied up in knots, and he kept seeing Nina's fragile shoulders as they tensed against him, saw her biting her lip to keep from crying.

Luckily he got the producers and stagehands back on the same page. It looked like the show would go on, just barely thanks to him.

He got back to his apartment around three, but as soon as he opened the door, the whole ugly scene from the morning washed over him and he felt sick.

Last night her husky voice had whispered how good he made her feel, and today he'd made her cry. He could still see her face pale when he spoke to her, the way her fingers had clenched around his robe, pulling it tighter as if in defense.

But he'd ignored all that. He'd needed to get on with his day.

He hadn't meant to act like he was paying her off. He'd just wanted to give her money for a cab, and didn't have anything smaller than a fifty-dollar bill.

He had to tell her he was sorry. His hands shook a little as he dialed her number, but it went straight to voicemail. He tried several more times over the next few hours and it was the same thing. She must have turned her phone off.

The thing was, he'd really hoped to see her again if she ever came to town. Their chemistry was amazing, he just had to keep things under control, not get too carried away. He could do that, couldn't he? Of course, none of that would be an issue if she never spoke to him again.

He wouldn't blame her if she didn't accept his apology, but he had to try. He'd just have to man up and go see her in person. Not pausing even to call the car service, he headed out the door.

***

Nina hardly ever took cabs. They were an indulgence she couldn't afford, but this morning had been a special kind of hell, and she deserved the privacy of her own car.

She managed not to cry on the ride home, but just barely. The five floors to her apartment seemed longer and steeper than ever. She was sore and rubbery from all the sex, which would have been a pleasurable reminder if it hadn't turned so awful.

Stacy's door was closed, so she was probably still asleep. The restaurant she worked at stayed open all night, so she often didn't get home until early morning.

Nina headed straight for her own room where she shed her clothes as quickly as possible and threw them in the corner. She put on comfy yoga pants and a sweatshirt and fell exhausted into bed.

She was vaguely aware of Stacy opening the door at some point and asking if she was all right, but she wasn't even sure if she answered her out loud. Hunger and a full bladder finally drove her out of bed at three o'clock.

She staggered to the bathroom and met Stacy on the way out. She must have looked pretty awful because her friend looked at her with concern.

"You okay, Neen?"

A few minutes later she was telling Stacy the whole story while snuggled under an afghan on their saggy old couch.

"Wow, that is so cold," Stacy said when she'd finished. "That bastard. I'll kick his ass if I ever see him again."

"It was just so Jekyll and Hyde, you know? Up until this morning, everything was amazing. He was amazing. I'd never have believed he could act that way. But obviously I don't know him."

"I'm so sorry. This is all my fault. I should never have introduced you."

"Don't be silly," Nina said. "You didn't make me sleep with the man. Anyway, it's over and done with. Good riddance to him."

"Amen," Stacy replied.

Neither one had much to say after this, and they fell into a glum silence, one interrupted a minute later by the sudden buzzing of the outside intercom.

Nina and Stacy looked at one another. "Maybe China Gourmet read our minds and is delivering us takeout," Stacy said, heaving herself off the couch. "Yes?" she said into the speaker.

A familiar voice spoke, somewhat distorted but still recognizable. Ian.

"I'd like to see Nina. Is she there?"

"She doesn't want any, Ian. Have a nice life."

The buzzer went off twice more but they grimly ignored it.

When it had been quiet for a couple of minutes, Stacy turned to Nina. "Since China Gourmet doesn't seem to be reading minds today, how about I give them a call?"

"Totally," Nina agreed, giving her a shaky smile.

Stacy placed their order and they turned on the TV and watched a re-run of Top Chef, letting themselves get seriously hungry as a lead-up to their big pig-out. When the buzzer shrilled thirty minutes later Stacy looked around for her shoes so she could meet the guy half-way up. They always felt bad making delivery guys climb all the way.

She'd only found one shoe before there was a knock on the door.

"Wow, that was fast," Nina said, holding her money over her head without taking her eyes off the TV. There were only three minutes left in the challenge and the chefs had to make a meal with vanilla beans, lobster, polenta and green chiles.

"What the hell are you doing here?" she heard Stacy say.

Nina turned around, her heart stopping at the sight of Ian standing in the doorway. He was holding a bag of Chinese food and looking distinctly uncomfortable in the face of Stacy's wrath.

"I need to talk to Nina," he said, his tone conciliatory and defensive at the same time.

"From what I understand, you said plenty earlier. You don't deserve another chance with her."

Ian flinched as if slapped in the face.

"No, I probably don't, but Nina deserves an apology." He was looking at Nina now. "I'd like to give her one if I could."

Stacy turned around and looked at Nina questioningly. Nina looked over at Ian, watching him, gauging her feelings. He shifted restlessly from one foot to the other, flushing under her scrutiny.

"I'll talk to him," she said, and saw him visibly relax.

"I'll take that," Stacy said, shooting Ian a warning glare before grabbing the greasy paper bag from him and heading into her bedroom. She turned around and shot Nina a reassuring smile and then disappeared through the doorway.

Ian remained by the door, as if waiting for permission to enter. Let him stay there. She really didn't want him any closer than that at the moment. Her only concession was to mute the TV and turn a bit on the couch so that she was facing him.

"Go ahead. Say what you came to say."

"I just wanted you to know..." He stopped and dragged a hand through his hair, then shoved both hands into his coat pockets. It hit her then that he looked awful. Still beautiful, because unfortunately he wasn't capable of looking unattractive, but also haggard and unhappy.

Nina waited in silence and let him struggle. No way was she going to help him through this.

He tried again. "I can't tell you how sorry I am for how I acted this morning. I had an incredible time with you. You're amazing, and I don't know what was wrong with me to treat you that way." He paused a moment, glancing at her as if to judge her reaction before continuing. "If someone had treated my sister like that, I'd have wanted to kill him," he said, his voice lower now and filled with self-loathing. "The thing is, I really wanted to see you again. Before you left or when you came back to visit. I still do, but I understand if that's off the table."

Nina listened, trying to keep herself from feeling anything, from showing any reaction. But finally she couldn't keep silent.

"You made me feel like a fool," she said quietly.

"Oh, Nina," he said, his voice anguished, and then he was kneeling in front of her. "I'm so sorry, baby." His hands were in her hair, cradling her face. He kissed her forehead, her cheeks. He grabbed her hands in his and leaned his forehead against hers.

He drew an uneven breath. "Will you come out with me tonight? Just for a little while? I'll buy you dinner or coffee. Whatever you want. Or we could just walk a little if you'd rather."

What did she want? She wanted to believe he was sorry and wouldn't hurt her again. She wanted more of what he'd made her feel before. But maybe he wasn't the man he'd seemed to be.

"I'm not sure I can trust you again," she whispered.

Ian sucked in a breath and his hands clenched tighter around hers. He drew back a little and looked at her as if she were already lost to him.

"I'll leave you alone then," he said, his voice rough with suppressed feeling. He released her hands and stood up, giving her one last pained look before turning toward the door.

She should let him go. There was no reason on earth to go back for more, especially when she was leaving so soon. But reason had nothing to do with it.

"Actually, I could use a walk," she said.

He turned around, his eyes wide with surprise and hope.

"Really? That's great! I can come back after you've eaten dinner. Would that be better?"

"Let me just check with Stacy."

His face fell. "She'll probably tie you up to keep you from coming with me, but okay. I'll wait here."

Stacey's door was open a crack, probably the better to hear them. Nina knocked lightly and stepped inside. Her friend was sitting on the bed surrounded by several opened cartons of Chinese food.

"Did you get all of that?" Nina whispered, sitting down beside her.

"Hell, yes. I'm sorry but I had to know if any ass-kicking was required." She sighed. "I suppose you might as well go with him. He was pretty convincing with the groveling, and I guess if you like him it's worth at least ending it on a good note. Besides, I've eaten most of the food, so you should make him take you out to dinner."

"Thanks, Stacy. I really appreciate you being there for me today."

"Don't sweat it. I'd do anything for you. I just wish you weren't leaving."

Now they both had tears in their eyes. Nina gave Stacy a quick hug and stood up.

"Ian's probably sweated right through his shirt by now, which serves him right. But I feel better now, and I may just go to dinner after all. Don't feel like you have to wait around if you have big plans tonight."

"All right. Have a good time."

Nina went into her own room and tossed her clothes around until she came up with her favorite jeans. She threw on a chocolate brown ribbed turtleneck since she was still feeling protective and anyway, she wasn't angling to show Ian cleavage he didn't deserve. She pulled on a pair of sexy brown suede ankle boots currently on loan from Stacy, ran a brush through her hair and went back into the living room.

Ian was still standing by the door, as if afraid to move without permission, and he looked unbearably tense. As soon as she smiled at him his hunched shoulders relaxed and he beamed at her.

"You look incredible. Ready?"

There was no way she looked incredible, not after the day she'd had, but he got points for effort. Grabbing her purse and no-nonsense black pea coat, she proceeded him down the stairs into the chilly evening. Ian smiled down at her, his expression oddly tender.

"Where to?" he asked.

As soon as he asked her stomach gave a low growl, reminding her that she hadn't eaten anything all day. Not even breakfast.

"Actually, I wouldn't mind dinner, if that's okay. I'm pretty hungry."

"Great! Me too," he said. "What would you like?"

"There's this amazing Ukrainian diner just a couple blocks away, if you want to give that a try."

"You mean Veselka's?" he asked, clearly surprised. "I love that place. I almost cried the first time I had their stuffed cabbage."

Nina smiled at him, relieved that they might be able to bypass any awkwardness. "Maybe we'll even see someone famous. I've seen a few lesser-known actors there this past year."

"Yeah, I saw Newman from *Seinfeld* there one day," he said, taking her hand in his as they headed down the sidewalk. "But I played it cool."

Then he seemed to realize what he'd done because he stopped in his tracks and looked down at their joined hands, then at her.

"In this okay?" he asked.

"Yes, this is good," Nina replied, smiling at him.

His answering smile had just a touch of wickedness in it, and Nina's breath caught in her throat. Good lord, had she ever stood a chance against this man?

The restaurant was busy, as usual, so they stood in front of the dessert case debating the merits of various pies and cakes until they were seated.

Their waitress, a middle-aged woman in blue eye shadow, false eyelashes and a leopard print dress, came to their table.

"What can I get you, hon?" she asked Nina, writing down her order. Then she turned to Ian and raised her eyebrows. "What about you, hot stuff?" she asked, her pencil at the ready, and Nina had the pleasure of seeing Ian blush.

"I don't even know where you grew up," Nina said after the waitress left.

"Closter, New Jersey," Ian answered. "Not too exciting, but decent enough."

Closter was a well-to-do suburb commuting distance to Manhattan. It was just as she suspected; Ian had grown up very comfortably.

"You must have come into the city a lot as a kid then, huh?"

"My dad was city comptroller for three terms, so for a while he commuted here every day. He's retired now and just donates his services to a couple local charities. Other than that he plays a lot of golf, the usual retired guy stuff. My mom's a pediatrician. We always came into the city, so I've always felt pretty at home here, but I went to the West Coast for school."

"Let me guess. Berkeley?"

"Stanford."

Nina smiled, glad to have a sense of where he came from. Both parents sounded like pretty impressive people, so it was no wonder Ian was so successful, not to mention comfortable in outrageously expensive restaurants.

He looked expensive, too, but not in an obnoxious, over the top way. He just looked like a guy who knew how to dress. Tonight he wore a baby blue button down shirt that matched his eyes over perfectly tailored black trousers. The gorgeous chrome watch on his wrist was nothing to sneeze at either.

Of course, she'd also seen him in Nike track pants and a worn tee shirt and he looked just as spectacular. And that wasn't anything compared to what he looked like naked, lying in bed with that look in his eye...

"So what brought you back to New York?" she asked, trying to stay focused on the conversation even as she felt herself heating up.

"I was pretty sure I wanted to go to law school but I wanted to live a little first, so I went to Alaska and worked the fisheries there with some buddies. After that I applied to law schools and then did the typical European tour while I waited to hear if I got in anywhere. A year later I was at Yale."

He leaned back in his chair and regarded her. "Now you know all there is to know about me."

Nina laughed and took a sip of water. "Somehow I doubt that, but it's a good start."

***

It was after ten when the waitress gave them the eye for taking up precious table space while people were still waiting in line. Reluctantly they left and headed back to her apartment, both of them quieter now. Ian insisted on seeing her to her door, so together they climbed the five flights and stopped outside her apartment.

"Thanks for dinner," she said, suddenly nervous. "That was really nice."

"I'm just glad you agreed to come out with me."

"I'm glad too," she said, feeling awkward and ridiculous, like a teenager on a first date.

But it wasn't just her. Ian was definitely lingering, like he didn't want to go just yet.

"So you're still leaving Wednesday morning?" he asked.

"Yes, that's the plan."

Good lord, why did he have to be so outrageously sexy? He'd felt so good on top of her, inside her, all that strength, those sleek muscles. Everything in her wanted to ask him in, but that was crazy. It was late and tomorrow was Monday. The time for sexcapades was over. Besides, the last thing she wanted was to put herself out there and get rejected again.

"You will come back and visit, right?" he asked.

"I hope so. I'm sure I'll need to get away before too long."

"Good. You should call me when you're coming."

"Sure. Okay," she agreed.

It was time to call it a night. Turning to the door she dug around in her purse for her key.

It wasn't there.

"Dammit, it must be in here," she said, embarrassed at the amount of junk floating around her purse.

Ian raised his eyebrows but waited patiently as she crouched on the floor and took out her wallet, make-up bag, planner and sketchbook. Still nothing, but maybe Stacy was home.

Nina knocked several times, each time louder than the last, but there was no sound from within. She was now flushed and thoroughly mortified, frantically looking through her things yet again. She called Stacy on her cell phone, but there was no answer.

"This never happens. I always put my keys right back in this pocket when I get home. I guess I just wasn't thinking straight this morning..." Her voice trailed off as she realized how much she'd just revealed.

Ian looked wounded, as if the hurt he'd caused her pained him as well.

"No problem. You can come home with me," he said, as if it were no big deal.

Nina's heart jumped into her throat. How many ups and downs could she have in one day with this man?

"That's not necessary. I can wait at the bar around the corner."

"Don't be ridiculous. I'm not leaving you here to sit in a bar all night."

She bit her lip, agonizing over whether to go with him. "I don't want to impose."

He gave her a look. "Are you kidding me? All night I've been wishing I could get you back to my place. You have no idea how glad I am you don't have your key."

Nina's mouth fell open and she offered no resistance when he took her hand and led her back downstairs.

"Why no car tonight?" she asked him. "Not that I mind slumming in a taxi."

Ian slanted a look at her. "I was too impatient to see you to wait around for it."

Nina just looked at him, unable to think what to say. The man was constantly knocking her off balance.

Ian hailed a cab and held the door open as she climbed in. They were both quiet on the drive uptown, the awareness between them as keen as ever, only now it was more complicated. The last two nights they'd both known why she was coming back. Tonight was a whole other story.

Or was it?

They entered his building and stepped into the elevator. As soon as the doors shut they looked at one another, trying to take the other's measure. The tension increased as they left the elevator and entered his apartment. Before she realized what he was doing he was behind her, helping her off with her coat. His hands brushed her neck, sending a bolt of lust straight to her belly, and she gasped audibly.

Ian stilled behind her and she felt his heat, sensed his coiled muscles only inches away.

"Nina," he breathed, his voice rough with need.

Slowly she turned around and met his gaze, and the intensity she saw there burned through her fear. Then he was kissing her, his hands in her hair, his mouth slanting over hers as she opened for him, the emotions of the day lending an urgency to their coming together.

This time she led the way to his room. They fell into bed, rolling over it as they wrestled for control. The hurt and confusion of the day, the unknowns that still lay before them, turned their need to near desperation.

Nina straddled him and her hands roamed greedily, making him pay for what he'd made her feel that morning. Leaning forward she lowered herself onto him, her head falling back as he filled her. He bucked beneath her and his big hands gripped her hips, but he made no move to take over as she rode him.

Her body was coiled tight, her eyes closed as she focused on her own pleasure. Reaching down she touched herself exactly as she needed, coming apart with a sob. Ian wrapped his arms around her and thrust twice, his body arcing upwards as he called her name.

They lay there for several long minutes, Nina spent and pliant on top of Ian's big body, his heart pounding beneath her ear. His hand stroked her back and played with her hair, and before she could stop it, the thought came to her that she never wanted to leave.

She looked at Ian, amused and pleased with how utterly replete he looked. His eyes were closed, his face relaxed. In another minute or two he'd probably be asleep.

"You just about killed me, woman."

"They don't call it a little death for nothing," she replied, more than a little proud of her performance.

He laughed softly and planted a sweet kiss on her lips.

"I'm glad you came back."

"Me too," she said.

She gave him one more peck and then slipped off of him. When she came back from the bathroom he was dead asleep. Smiling, she slid in beside him.

Chapter Four

"Ian, wake up. You overslept," Nina said, shaking his shoulder.

Ian opened his eyes and stared groggily at her.

"What? What's wrong?" he said sitting up with a worried look.

"It's after nine. You're late for work," she said urgently.

Ian flopped back onto his pillow. "It's Columbus Day. The office is closed."

"Oh, sorry," Nina said, embarrassed to have woken him up for no reason. "Never mind, then. Go back to sleep."

Ian's arm shot out and he dragged her down next to him. "Now I'm awake and must be appeased."

"Can that wait until after we eat? I'm kind of starving."

She went to pull his robe off its hook, but a flicker of anxiety rose in her.

"Is it okay if I wear this?" she asked.

"Of course you can. You don't need to ask. But must you wear anything?" he asked, looking at her lecherously.

"I must," she said, arching an eyebrow at him as she tried to suppress a smile.

She put it on, breathing in his lingering scent.

"Want me to start the coffee?" she asked over her shoulder.

"God, yes."

Though this was the third morning she'd stayed over, she had yet to get a good look at the whole apartment. Now she took her time as she made for the kitchen, poking her head into various rooms.

One room was being used as an office. A huge modern desk sat in front of a window and a big comfy armchair was set against the left-hand wall, a standing lamp beside it. On the opposite wall were the beginnings of what looked to be a do-it-yourself bookshelf project. Boards of various sizes, all stained walnut, were piled together and a toolbox and drill kit sat nearby, waiting for action.

Ian come up beside her, yawning hugely. He'd put on a pair of brown cords and a green and brown flannel shirt. His dark hair was mussed and adorable and he had the hint of a beard along his jaw.

Yum.

"It's going to be fantastic when I'm done," he told her, obviously proud. "That whole wall will be bookshelves."

"Wow, that's quite a project," she said. "I guess you must have loads of time to kill in between working weekends and training for triathlons."

Ian laughed and shrugged his shoulders. "I get restless if I'm not doing something. Gets me out of my head too. Of course, you can only have so many bookshelves, but I do things for my parents, too. Strip furniture, that kind of thing."

"See, I really don't get that. I could sit around with a book for hours. It's a good thing there are people like you in the world. Otherwise people like me would be sitting around in the dark, wondering how to make fire."

"People like me are happy to keep the lights on for people like you," he said, giving her a quick kiss. "Now how about we get that coffee going?"

Ian was a deft hand at omelet-making and refused to let Nina help. Instead she sat at the kitchen table and watched him, which was no hardship. In no time at all he was serving a perfect, fluffy spinach and cheese omelet along with half a grapefruit and two slices of toast.

It was a far cry from yesterday morning.

"I guess I've probably thrown your training schedule off," she said around mouthfuls. "Is that bad?"

"I'll get back at it tomorrow. My next race isn't until February, but it's a tough one and I really want to improve my time."

"I can't even imagine being able to do that. I run sometimes, but it's never even occurred to me to push myself that way," she said, digging into her grapefruit and trying not to squirt herself in the eye.

"You push yourself in your art, right? People do it in different ways. I was always a hyper kid. Sometimes I drove my mother so crazy she'd send me outside to run around the house until I wore myself out. I guess it stuck."

Nina smiled at the image of him as a little boy circling his house, his little feet flying. "I'd love to see you race someday," she said, the words out before she had time to censure them.

Ian didn't seem to think it so strange though. His eyes widened with surprise and then a grin appeared. "That'd be great. Maybe you can come back to visit for the next one."

Nina smiled at him, pleased and confused at the same time. She hadn't forgotten yesterday, and couldn't help worrying about when she ought to leave. As soon as they were done eating she got up from the table and put her dishes in the sink.

"I probably should get going," she said, forcing a cheerful smile. "It's getting kind of late..."

"Already? I was hoping you'd stay a while."

"Oh, I just figured..."

He looked stricken. "You figured I was such an asshole yesterday, you were afraid to stick around and see when I'd become one again."

Nina bit her lip and said nothing.

Ian stood up and came over to her, cupping her face in his hands as he looked at her, his eyes dark and serious.

"I'd really like you to stay, Nina. I promise you the jerk you saw yesterday will never come back."

"Okay," she said, a long breath escaping her. "I'd like that."

After a long and steamy shower together they headed downtown to do the kinds of touristy things people never did when they actually lived in New York. But Ian considered it a sin for her to leave without seeing the top of the Empire State Building, and after that they rode the Staten Island Ferry and had reubens and egg cream sodas at a deli on the Lower East Side.

"I really ought to go home," Nina said as they left the deli. "I've been in these clothes an awfully long time now."

"As I see it, we have two viable options. We stop at your place and get some clothes so you can come back with me, or we go buy you some clothes and you come back with me. Actually, there's a third option. We go straight back to my place and you don't wear any clothes."

A thrill of delight raced up her spine. She'd just had the best day of her life, and the only thing marring it was the thought that it had to end. But maybe it didn't. The only hitch was that she and Stacy had seen so little of one another, and soon she'd be leaving. She didn't want to be one of those women who ditched a friend for a guy.

"I really do need to go home. Stacy kind of set tonight and tomorrow aside so we could hang. But it's not even four yet, so she's not home for another couple of hours. Why don't we go to my place for a bit?" she suggested, wriggling her eyebrows in case he didn't catch her meaning.

"Very subtle, sweetheart. Don't worry, I'm right behind you."

She was self-conscious after having spent so much time in his much nicer apartment, but by the time they got inside neither of them was paying much attention to the décor.

They fell naked onto her clothes-strewn bed. Stretching, she rummaged through her wobbly nightstand and came up with a condom packet. She checked the date. Not expired, thank the good lord.

Ian rolled on top of her and kissed her senseless. Then he looked around her room, at the suitcases and garbage bags, the empty closet. "You should stay a little while longer."

"You mean like for dinner?" she asked, trying not to look too pleased that he'd asked. She lifted her hips, unable to keep from touching him in every possible way.

"No, I mean stay in New York a few more weeks. It would be like a vacation."

Nina stared up at him. "But I can't. Stacy's already got someone moving in next week."

"You could stay at my place," he said, grinning wickedly before leaning down to kiss her neck. It was nearly impossible for her to think with him all around her, his heat and desire stoking her own. "We could have sex like this every day, eat like kings, see a few shows. What could be bad?"

She couldn't do that, could she? Just stay here, with this man she barely knew?

"I don't know..."

"Do you need to be in New Hampshire for something?" he asked.

"Not exactly, but..."

"Come on, Nina. It'll be fun. You could relax and enjoy the city without all the usual worries. Every day could be like today."

"What if we realize we can't stand each other?"

"Then you leave, same as before. You've got nothing to lose. I don't know about you, but what we have here doesn't happen every day. Not to me, anyway."

Nina was silent, her mind frantically trying to examine all the pros and cons. However long she stayed, it would still have to end, whether it was now or in a few weeks. But there was no denying it was a tempting proposition.

Ian made another pitch.

"If you leave now I'll compare every woman I meet to you, and none of them will ever be able to compete. You'll have doomed every future relationship, in effect ruining the rest of my life. We have to let this run its course so we can have some mediocre sex, get sick of each other and go our separate ways."

"You're ridiculous," she said, but the feel of him on top of her was too much. She writhed beneath him, running her hands down his back until she was gripping his ass.

"Ridiculously hot for you," he said, leaning down and taking her nipple in his mouth.

Wrapping her legs around his hips she rose up, urging him toward her, making it clear she was ready. With a low laugh he slid over her, back and forth, working her into a frenzy.

"Ian," she said, desperate for him.

"Not so fast, baby." Again he slid over her.

She was so wet now he could have slipped right inside her. Again she lifted her hips in invitation. He groaned but didn't take the bait. He kissed her full and deep, drinking her in, his tongue moving in rhythm with his cock until every nerve ending was alive with need.

"Please, Ian."

"Tell me you'll stay," he said, holding himself over her, the muscles in his arms taut and beautifully defined, his eyes fierce on hers as once again he slid over her. He was killing her, but she was getting to him, too. His arms trembled and his cock throbbed against her.

"Yes. I'll stay. I'll stay," she cried out.

As soon as the words were out he put the condom on. Then he was kissing her again, deep drugging kisses as he slid inside her, filling her completely. Her legs came up, taking him even deeper, and he groaned in satisfaction, holding her legs against his chest.

"God, yes. Harder," she demanded, and he let loose, plowing into her as the tide rose in her and she rose and rose, trembling on the peak until she broke apart around him, crying out and clutching his arms as she shuddered.

***

"Wow," Stacy said. "I mean, wow."

They were sitting on the sofa eating take-out. Thai food this time.

"Yeah, I know. It's probably totally insane, but I couldn't say no. Anyway, I'm not in such a rush to go home."

"I'd probably do the same thing if I were in your shoes. I just hope he treats you right."

"If he doesn't I can always leave."

"Do you think you might be falling for him?" Stacy asked, her expression full of concern.

"Right now I'm so dazed with lust and sexual satisfaction, I don't know what to call it. I'll let you know when I do."

"Well at least I won't lose you yet. I can feel grateful to him for that," Stacy said, smiling a little now, though the worry hadn't left her eyes.

"That's right. And I'll be a woman of leisure, so anytime you want to do lunch, just let me know."

"Deal," Stacy said, smiling for real now. She picked up the remote and aimed it at the TV. "Let's see what crazy shit the cooks have to make this time."

***

As promised, Ian showed up in the town car at seven o'clock the next evening to bring her and her things back to his place. Stacy had agreed to keep a few boxes in a closet, so Nina brought only a couple of suitcases, a box of books and sketchbooks and her painting supplies, such as they were.

She tried to think of it as if she were staying at a hotel. It was just as impermanent, just as casual. Even so, it felt oddly intimate to put her toothbrush in the same holder as Ian's. He had a guest room with a chest of drawers and a closet that held only a few coats, so she put her things in there, but she still couldn't shake the feeling that she was intruding. So often, she'd been the one to want more than her boyfriends. Now, even though staying was his idea, she still half expected him to change his mind.

She finished unpacking her things to find him in the kitchen, cooking something that smelled amazing.

"What's for dinner?" she asked, trying to act casual.

"Nothing fancy. Salmon and roasted veggies, plus a salad."

"Mmm. Anything I can do?" she asked.

"Just keep me company."

"Are you going to be this easy on me the whole time I'm here?" she asked teasingly.

"Probably. You make me want to spoil you."

Her heart stuttered and sped up. She said nothing for several minutes, too surprised to reply.

"So have you ever lived with a woman before?" The question was out before she realized how un-casual it would sound. "Not that we're living together now," she added quickly, further mortifying herself.

Ian smiled, as if amused by her anxious self-correcting. "Yeah, for a little while," he said, expertly cutting vegetables on a beautiful piece of wood.

It was one of those cutting boards made from one slice of a tree and probably cost as much as her monthly rent had been. She watched, transfixed by the sight of his big, capable hands working so nimbly.

"It was a few years ago now. I guess I thought living together would fix some of the problems we were having, but all it did was make them more obvious."

"What problems?" Nina asked, curious. There was a sliver of something like jealously, but mostly she wanted more insight into this man she still barely knew.

"Karen thought I worked too much and didn't spend enough time with her. She said I always picked work over her. She was right, I did, and I don't blame her for minding. I wanted to make partner and I worked my ass off seven days a week. It didn't leave much time for anything else, including my relationship."

"You must have slowed down a little since you made partner," Nina pointed out. "I've seen an awful lot of you in the last few days."

Ian stopped abruptly and looked up, clearly surprised by her comment. He smiled wolfishly at her. "I guess I must be more excited about you. I can't remember ever running home so I could be with her."

A rush of heat spread through her at the idea of him running home from work to see her. "Don't worry, I won't expect you to cut back for me," Nina said, opening the cabinet just above her to find the plates.

She couldn't just stand around uselessly, and this conversation, which she herself had started, was making her antsy. Pulling down two plates, she walked over to the table in the adjoining room and set them out.

"I can't promise I'll leave right at five o'clock while you're here, but you'd better believe you'll be seeing me. If you're only here for a few weeks, I'm going to take advantage."

"You do that," she said, giving him an exaggerated look and a flutter of her eyelashes.

Ian was as good as his word, taking advantage for hours that night, so much so that she barely remembered him getting ready for work the next morning. She came awake slowly hours later, smiling as she recalled where she was. She couldn't remember ever having more than a day at a time with nothing to do except enjoy herself. It was glorious, and a little unnerving as well.

Then it hit her. She'd never had a vacation.

Not once since the age of eighteen had she had any extra money to go away with friends, nor had she had the luxury of taking time off of work. Now here she was for three weeks, and all she had to do was be a good houseguest.

Of course, she still didn't have enough money to do much while she was here, but at least she wouldn't have to work. Too bad she didn't have any money for painting supplies. Since getting out of school she'd never had enough time to paint, to experiment and follow an idea through without interruption or running out of materials.

She was sipping her coffee and reading the *Times* when she heard her phone ring from the bedroom and ran to answer it. Her mother.

"Hi Mom," she said, trying not to sound disappointed. She'd been hoping it was Ian, though there was no reason to think he would call her.

"Thank goodness you answered. I've been trying to reach you ever since I got your message. Please tell me you're not serious about staying another three weeks."

"Actually, I am serious, Mom."

"Nina, you can't simply change your plans on a whim. People depend on you to keep your word. Mrs. Lamb needs a hand now that she's back from the hospital, and I told her you'd help until you found a job. I'm sure she'd pay a little something. I know what you're thinking, but beggars can't be choosers."

"I didn't give my word to Mrs. Lamb, and you had no business promising her on my account. I have a lot to figure out when I get back."

"Oh Nina, what's to figure out? You'll come back here and get a job like everyone else. Unless you want to get your MBA. Your father and I would help pay for it."

Nina bit back a reply, knowing it was no use. She'd heard it all before, but it still hurt that after all these years her parents didn't get it. She'd be paying off her student loans until she was fifty, had gone days eating nothing but tuna and ramen noodles, and her mother had never once offered to help her with anything except tuition for a business degree.

"I have to go now. Do me a favor and don't arrange any other jobs for me."

"Now Nina, don't give me that attitude –"

"Bye, Mom," she said, and hung up.

She let her head fall into her hands, despair seeping through her. She'd been a fool to think she could survive moving back. It was a good thing she had some time to think through her next move, because there was no way in hell she was going home.

What she needed was to find an apartment she could share for a few hundred a month and get back on her feet. It really didn't matter where it was, so long as she found a job to cover the bills.

A few minutes later she was on her laptop and logging into Facebook, checking out friends from school to see who was where. She wrote to about a dozen people to let them know she was in the market for a new job, posted her situation on her wall, and then closed her computer and looked around. It was nearly noon and she was sitting in a man's apartment, unwashed, hungry and a little desperate about her future. She needed to get some fresh air.

She was in and out of the shower in record time and dressed in jeans and turtleneck sweater, her worn leather jacket thrown over it all. Grabbing her canvas bag she threw in a few pencils, some charcoal and her sketchbook – at least she could still afford those – took the key Ian had left her and headed out the door.

It was another clear and perfect fall day, and she felt better as soon as she got outside. Everyone looked so happy, but maybe that's just how people looked on the Upper West Side.

She spent the rest of the morning roaming the neighborhood, then walked across the park to the Met. She'd long since memorized the city's museum admission fees, particularly their free days. Some, like the Met, were "pay what you wish" all the time, which was pretty fantastic. Of course she *wished* she could pay the full price, but instead she paid what she could afford, which today was three dollars.

Even now, after a year of visiting museums, a burning knot of shame flared when she got to the teller and handed her money over. God knew she wasn't the only poor artist in the city, so she really should have gotten over it, but it didn't seem to want to let her go.

Since she had the luxury of going regularly, she generally liked to confine her visits to one wing, the better to absorb what she was seeing. Sometimes she spent a couple hours looking at just two or three paintings. Today, needing the solace, she went straight to her favorite room in the Asian wing. Dim and cool, with pillars set in rows near the entrance, it was designed to feel like a garden or temple. In that atmosphere her mind also quieted and she let her pencil flow over paper as she drew various urns from the cases built into the wall.

It was almost like meditation, the way her mind emptied of all but her work, her focus clear and directed. A kind of euphoric calm descended over her, leaving her tired but refreshed when she finally closed her sketchbook and looked up hours later.

Leaving the museum she breathed deeply and looked around, taking in the people around her in all their variety. It really was an amazing city when it wasn't beating you down.

Inspired to make dinner as well as art, she stopped in a little grocery and spent more than a few precious dollars on the makings for her signature lasagna. It was four-thirty when she got back to the apartment, and she soon had a pan cooking in the oven.

She was busy throwing a salad together when Ian came home. Her heart actually leapt in her chest at the sound, but she made herself stay where she was. No way was she running to greet him at the door.

"Wow, something smells delicious," he said, coming into the kitchen. He was smiling with delight and looking gorgeous, a wealthy man-about-town in his suit and trench coat.

"I hope you like lasagna, because that's what's for dinner."

"Does anyone not like lasagna? Anyway, I'd love whatever you made. But I don't want you to feel like you need to cook for me."

"I'm not cooking for you, I'm cooking for us."

"Well, in that case," he murmured, pulling her toward him.

Nina threw her arms around his neck and pressed against him, wishing there wasn't so much clothing between them. Leaning down he kissed her. A slow, exploring kiss that had her going in seconds.

"How long before dinner's ready?" he asked in between kissing her neck.

"Uh, half an hour," she said, already breathless.

"Then we'd better get moving," he said, breaking the kiss and pulling her into his room.

When they finally sat down to dinner, Nina was wearing his robe and he was wearing sweats. They were rumpled and flushed, not to mention ravenous.

"This is amazing," he said, eating with gusto. "You're amazing."

Nina just smiled, feeling herself flush with pleasure at the warmth in his eyes. They spent the rest of dinner filling one another in on their day. Afterwards Ian insisted on cleaning up. "It's only fair," he said, shooing her away. "Don't worry, your time will come."

Laughing, Nina retreated to the plush blue sofa in the living room and opened her sketchbook. When he was done in the kitchen Ian joined her on the sofa with a legal thriller.

It was surprisingly cozy and domestic, and she couldn't help smiling to herself. She'd been worried about what they'd do when they weren't screwing each other senseless, but maybe she'd been worried for nothing.

Ian got up at six-thirty the next morning to go for a run. Nina briefly considered joining him – for the first fifteen feet anyway, since after that he would have left her in the dust – and then promptly fell back asleep. She woke up again to see him standing in front of his closet, a towel wrapped around his waist. His hair was damp, his muscles gleamed.

God have mercy.

He must have heard her little moan because he turned around and looked at her, a smile spreading over his face.

Nina sat up on an elbow, accidentally on purpose letting the sheet fall to her waist. "Just hypothetically, would a man who just ran fifteen miles have any energy left for ravishing?"

"Hell, yes," he said, letting his towel hit the floor.

Chapter Five

Thursday dawned clear and in the mid-fifties. Deciding to take advantage of the fine weather, Nina headed out at noon and meandered her way to Central Park, where she bought a pretzel and hotdog from a vendor. She ate quickly before sitting down on a bench, letting her mind wander and her hand fly as she sketched people she saw – quick, impressionistic drawings that caught the essence of the mothers with their kids, old men doing Tai Chi, joggers and inline skaters.

She really should draw Ian before she left. He'd make a great model with those long, toned muscles, so well defined without being bulky.

"Can you draw people so they look really funny, like with big noses and funny expressions?"

Nina looked up to see a boy of maybe eight standing in front of her, peering over her shoulder in an effort to see her drawing.

"You mean caricatures?" she asked.

His face lit up and he nodded vigorously. "Yeah! Can you do one of me? My Mom'll pay you."

Nina wasn't so sure about that. A harried looking woman and her distracted husband caught up to him and stood there frowning and breathing heavily.

"I'm so sorry. Is he bothering you?" the mother asked, her voice lilting with a southern accent. "I'm trying to teach him that he can't just walk up to strangers, but he gets so excited."

"That's all right, he wasn't bothering me," Nina replied, wondering if they'd move on soon or if she'd have to find another spot.

"She said she'd draw me," the boy told his mother. "But you have to pay her. Will you. Please? She'll make me look funny."

"You do caricatures, is that it?" the father said, looking at Nina with interest. "I've always gotten a kick out of those. How much do you charge?"

This was odd. She'd never done a caricature in her life, unless you counted the drawings she did of her teachers when she was a kid. Then again, why not spend a few minutes and make a little money? If she did a lousy job she wouldn't charge them.

"Sure," she said. "It'll be ten dollars a drawing."

Just like that, the dad pulled his wallet out of his pocket, opened it up and handed her a ten.

Nina positioned the boy on a rock a few feet away and studied him, noting the particular curl of his ears, his little ski-jump nose and big eyes, the cowlick in his hair. In a few minutes she'd whipped off a funny, inoffensive likeness and showed it to the family, all of whom smiled broadly and clapped their hands. The dad handed over twenty more dollars so she could do one of him and his wife.

A young couple passing by stopped to watch and asked her to draw them, and then more people came by after them, and soon she was chatting with bystanders like a seasoned street artist.

At five o'clock she closed her pad and headed back to Ian's apartment, two hundred and twenty dollars richer than when she'd entered the park. Twenty dollars more than her monthly student loan payment. Not bad for a few hours of work.

***

Ian let his menu fall to the table and sat back in his chair, staring at Nina in amazement. "Get out. You spent the afternoon drawing caricatures?"

"I will not get out," Nina laughed. "But I'll draw you sometime, if you like."

"As long as you don't draw me with a small penis. A man can take anything but that."

"You're such a guy. Anyway, if I draw you in the nude, you can be damn sure it won't be a joke. I'll draw you for real."

She let her eyes run over him, as if she were picturing him naked, and Ian felt his body heat up yet again.

"You keep looking at me like that and we're not going to make it through dinner," he warned.

He was like a freakin' teenager, his near-constant boner trying to upstage his brain whenever she was near.

Nina smiled innocently and looked back at her menu. "We have to make it through dinner. I'm starving."

He sighed heavily. "The thrill is gone. You used to want to jump my bones when I gave you my look."

Nina laughed. "Babe, I did jump your bones when you gave me your look. That's why I'm starving." She looked back down at the menu, all business. "In order to make up for coming home late, I propose you get the duck. I'll get the lamb but you'll let me have a few bites of your duck, which I want only a little less than the lamb."

Ian drank his wine and watched Nina as she worked out her strategy. She was so adorable as she contemplated the menu, looking up at him every so often to check that he was falling in line with her plan.

He couldn't remember feeling so sated, content and thrilled at the same time. It was kind of disconcerting, since he'd been sure the sex would get less exciting after a few days, or he'd get tired of her kooky artist ways. But there was no sign of that yet. He was more aroused by her all the time.

The waiter came and he ordered the duck, even though he'd have preferred the filet mignon, and then watched her savor both his meal and hers when it came. Her eyes closed and she moaned, the sound not unlike the noises she made in bed.

"So what's your plan for tomorrow?" he asked her, trying to take his mind off his throbbing erection.

"Actually, I thought I'd go back to the park and fleece more tourists. It was kind of fun, and it certainly beat painting dogs in vests. Of course, I can't do that forever without getting a license. But it'll be too cold in a few weeks to do it anyway."

Ian looked at her in surprise, his fork halfway to his mouth. Nina blanched in embarrassment, instantly flushing under his gaze.

"What am I thinking?" she laughed, the sound forced. "I won't be around that long. Guess I'm getting a little too used to the lap of luxury." She picked up her wine and gulped it down.

Ian didn't say anything at first and an awkward silence fell. He wasn't sure what to say, though. He, too, caught himself making plans as if she'd be around longer. That probably wasn't so strange, given how much they were enjoying each other. Still, it complicated matters, and he didn't want to lead her on. He was having a great time, but he wasn't ready to live with anyone.

"Why don't we just see how things go?" he said, trying to strike a neutral tone. The last thing he wanted was to hurt her feelings. "Who knows how we'll feel in two weeks?"

Nina smoothed the napkin on her lap over and over, as if she couldn't look at him. He watched, his stomach clenching, as she schooled her expression before looking up at him.

"Don't worry. I'm not going to squat at your place forever. I'm actually looking into other options for when I leave here. I've decided not to go back home after all. I've written to a bunch of people I know to get the word out. Something will come through, I'm sure."

Ian tried to sound enthusiastic and asked her where she was hoping to move, but he hated the thought that she might end up too far away to easily visit New York.

Visit him.

Their easy banter had vanished and a pall hung over them the rest of the meal. He watched Nina, wondering what she was thinking. Did she want to stay in New York, or was it just a slip of the tongue?

He needed to stop worrying about it. He'd enjoy their time together and deal with the rest when the time came for her to leave.

There was no point in rushing things. In another two weeks they might have grown tired of each other and transitioned into mediocre sex like he'd joked about.

Then he looked across the table at her. No way would he be tired of her in two weeks. He was just getting started.

When the check came Nina eyed it like she wanted to offer money or at least see how much it was. Which was ridiculous, since obviously it was his treat. He gave her a look meant to quell any notions she might have and grabbed the leather folder.

Aside from her polite thanks for the dinner they were both quiet on the way back to his place. She was obviously upset, but he couldn't tell if she was angry at him or just uncomfortable.

He had no idea what to do or say. When they got back to his place he worked for a while on the bookshelf, channeling his frustration as he measured and pieced things together. Hopefully it wasn't bothering Nina, but then again, it was his place, right? What was he supposed to do, tiptoe around her?

Nina walked by his office at one point, glancing in and giving him the barest hint of a smile, as if it were all she could manage, before heading down the hall. She'd shed her sexy outfit and was wearing a long-sleeved white shirt and a pair of red pajama bottoms. They probably weren't supposed to be sexy, but there was no disguising her gorgeous ass.

Ian sighed and sat back on his heels, annoyed, turned-on and frustrated. He hadn't known her long enough to understand these sorts of episodes, or know how to talk to her. Then again, he'd encountered the same thing with other women, so maybe it didn't even matter. When you were dealing with a woman, it was always a mystery. Each event was a new experience, fraught with hazards.

That's why men had man-caves. Of course, before Nina, his whole apartment had been a man-cave. As it would be again when she left.

He really was going to miss her. He missed her right now, and she was only in the other room.

Ian put down his screwdriver and left the sanctuary of his study to find her. There were the usual signs of her presence – her sketchbook and pack of pencils on the coffee table, a mug with a little bit of tea in the sink – but no Nina.

When he got to his bedroom he realized she was already in bed. The lights were out, but he could just make out her form under the blankets.

Huh.

Looking at the clock he saw it was after ten. He shouldn't have worked so long without saying anything to her.

He washed up and slid into bed, careful not to wake her, but once he was lying down he could tell she was still awake. The fact that she said nothing meant she was pretending she was asleep, which was annoying and also a serious bummer.

There was nothing lonelier than lying in bed next to someone and not speaking.

Fuck it.

Turning on his side he looped his arm around her waist and pulled her toward him. He heard her little gasp of surprise, and for a minute she held herself rigid against him, as if unable to relax, but slowly he felt the tension leave her. Soon she was soft and pliant in his arms, her body molded to his. His body reacted as it always did, instantly hard and ready for her. There was no way she didn't know it, but he wasn't going to make another move unless he knew she wanted it. Lucky for him, it didn't take long. Turning in his arms until she faced him, she brought her mouth to his.

This time there was a new flavor, a new feeling from her. When she kissed him there was an edge to it, and when he ran his hand down her side she grabbed him and led him to her already slick heat, holding him there until she was wild beneath him.

"Lick me," she said, pushing at his shoulders, her hips rising off the bed in demand.

Taking his time even as he felt her impatience, he made his way down her body until he was between her legs. He brushed his thumbs over her, opening her up, breathing on her quivering skin as if he had all the time in the world.

Her hands fisted in the sheets and she let out little mewls of desire and frustration. His desire skyrocketed, but he took his sweet time even as he craved sinking into her. Slowly, methodically, he worked her over, lapping her up until she was strung tight, her body arcing off the bed, her fingers in his hair, holding him to her.

She was a vortex, dark and seductive, and he gladly let himself fall in. But he let her hold nothing back; that was his price. For as long as she was here she was his. Every part of her. Lifting her hips, he thrust his tongue into her, her scent all around him like a drug.

"I need you. Now. Now, Ian," she cried.

He was more than ready. Pulling away, he dragged a condom on and settled between her thighs.

But before he could enter her she pushed him onto his back and straddled him. His head threatened to explode as she took him in, her slick depths squeezing his length until he was in an agony of pleasure.

His hands gripped her hips, trying to set the pace, but she was having none of it. He was desperate for release now, and a growl escaped him as he watched her touch herself. Pushing her hand away he replaced it with his own.

She let out a high keening wail as she came, her head thrown back as her body pulsed around him, setting off his own release. This time when he grabbed her hips he buried himself in her as the most intense orgasm he'd ever known swept over him.

He didn't exactly pass out, but his brain dimmed a bit, and it was a few minutes before he really came back to the living.

Nina was lying on him, her head resting on his chest. With great effort he reached up and stroked her silky hair, brushing it back from her forehead.

"You're still alive, then," she said, her voice husky.

"Just barely. But it wouldn't have been a bad way to go." He paused then, hesitant. "You okay, baby?"

"Better than okay. I guess I just..." She trailed off with a little sigh.

"It's all right. I think I get it," he said, rolling onto his side with her. Carefully he withdrew and pulled her close.

"Goodnight, Ian," she whispered, tucking herself into his side, her breath soft on his neck.

His chest tightened, something well beyond lust stirring in him as they lay skin to skin, breathing as one. Reluctant to examine this new, not so comfortable feeling, he closed his eyes and promptly fell asleep.

***

Nina woke the next morning when Ian was in the shower. Which was a relief, because she was feeling out of sorts after the night they'd had. Her emotions had been so raw they embarrassed her now. She felt hollowed out, as if only Ian were capable of filling her up with whatever he had to give, good or bad.

This was more than a casual affair now, for her at least. The waters had just gotten deeper, so deep she couldn't see the bottom.

Sliding out of bed, she fished her pajama bottoms and top off the floor and pulled them on before heading into the kitchen for a cup of coffee. Best to be fortified before seeing him.

She clutched her mug as she heard him get out of the shower. She'd felt last night that they'd had an understanding, but who knew what he would feel this morning?

"You're up early," he said, appearing at the kitchen door in his robe.

He was smiling and his eyes were bright and pleased as he came in and wrapped his arms around her. Leaning down he planted a kiss on her forehead. Relief flooded her as she smiled up at him, hugging him back.

She ran her fingers through his damp hair. "Mmm, you smell good. And you look like an Old Spice commercial."

He grinned and nuzzled her neck. "You smell delicious, but not store-bought delicious. Musky, sexy delicious."

"Whatever you say," Nina laughed, sucking in her breath as his mouth found hers for a lingering kiss.

He pulled away reluctantly. "I'd better get dressed. I have an early meeting today. Make sure you help yourself to a good breakfast. You'll need your strength if you're going to be fleecing tourists all day."

"If the weather holds and I can get out there a few more times, I'll have enough to buy some paints and canvas next week."

Ian looked at her for a moment, as if he were about to say something. Then he shook his head. "Knock 'em dead, tiger. I'll see you after work. Don't worry about dinner. I'll take care of it."

***

There were fewer tourists about due to the dropping temperature, and she only made fifty dollars in the six hours she was in the park. Aside from her lunch with Stacy, the day had dragged by.

By the time she got back to the apartment, Ian was already home.

"You're early," she said, smiling at him as she put her things down on a table and rubbed her hands together.

"Have you been out there all day?" he asked, frowning at her. "It's barely forty degrees out."

"You don't have to tell me that," she sighed. "There weren't as many people out today. I didn't make nearly as much as I'd hoped."

Ian took her chilled hands and chafed them between his, instantly warming them. "If you're up for it, I got tickets for American Ballet Theater tonight. It's their new choreographer showcase."

"Are you kidding? Of course I want to go," she squealed, hopping around in joy as Ian grinned at her. She loved the ballet, and it had been one of her real sorrows that she'd lived in a city with some of the best dance companies in the world and couldn't afford to see them. A thought occurred to her mid-hop and she stopped and looked at him. "I'm guessing you're not a huge ballet fan. Are you sure you want to go?" she asked, touched by the offer but a little worried he wouldn't enjoy himself.

"I admit I'd rather go to a Knicks game, but this'll be fun too. Anyway, you'll enjoy it, and that's what I was going for."

Throwing her arms around his neck she gave him a firm kiss on the lips. "I'd better shower and change then."

Not only did he take her to the show, they went to one of the finest restaurants in the city beforehand, though thankfully it wasn't as outrageous as Masa. It was exactly the kind of night she'd dreamed of having ever since coming to the city.

The rest of the weekend was equally perfect. Saturday afternoon they went to a movie and then for dim sum in Chinatown, where they debated the movie's merits and discovered they shared a passion for old thrillers like *The Big Heat* and *Gilda*. Sunday they had a double feature courtesy of Ian's DVD library, then spent the rest of the afternoon in bed making each other crazy.

It was without doubt the best weekend she'd ever had. She was sorry to see it end, but consoled herself that she'd have one or two more, depending on exactly when she left. But she wasn't going to think about leaving, not now. She was going to live in the moment if it killed her.

A somewhat restless night had her sleeping past nine Monday morning. She stumbled into the kitchen, so bleary-eyed it took her a full minute to register what she was seeing.

A yellow post-it note was stuck to the counter in front of the coffee maker. On it Ian had written in his confident, slanted hand: *Nothing should keep you from painting. Here's a little something to help you get started. Don't over-think it. – Ian*

Next to the note was a five hundred dollar gift card for New York Central Art Supply, the granddaddy of art supply stores. Sometimes she went in there just to look. She was like a guy in a porn shop, drooling over the rows and rows of paints and brushes, canvas and framing supplies. But in all the times she'd gone there, she'd never bought more than a few tubes of paint.

The thought of being able to buy five hundred dollars worth of supplies made her giddy. But then darker thoughts intruded, because of course she couldn't accept this kind of a gift.

Could she?

Desperate for some perspective, she texted Stacy asking her to call as soon as she woke up.

Not two minutes later Stacy called. "What's wrong?"

"Did I wake you? I'm sorry, I thought you kept your phone off –"

"Don't worry about it. I'm mostly awake, just kind of dozing in and out. What's up?"

Nina paced under the cathedral ceiling of Ian's living room as she filled her in. "It's just so weird, you know? I had insanely good sex with a gorgeous stranger a week ago, and now I'm staying with him and receiving extravagant gifts. Did I turn into a 'ho without realizing it?"

"Hold on a second. Let's slow down and think this through rationally, okay?" Stacy said. "First of all, is he making you *feel* like a whore?"

"Well, no," she said with a sigh. "It's just this gift card that's really throwing me."

"What did he say when he gave it to you? Was he like, 'Here babe, this is for being such a good lay,' or what?"

Nina laughed and sat down in an armchair facing the floor to ceiling windows, letting the golden autumn light warm her face.

"Of course not. His note just said that nothing should keep me from painting, and that I shouldn't over-think it."

"Oh, well, good thing you're not doing that."

"Can you blame me for being kind of flipped out?" she asked.

"No, no, I get it. And you shouldn't do anything that doesn't feel right. But this seems pretty innocent. He convinced you to stay and take a little vacation, and it'd be a shame if you couldn't paint during it. He seems to get that about you already. I say enjoy it. Live a little. If anyone deserves it, it's you, Nina."

"It really would be great to paint again, especially now that I have some time," she said, already picturing herself set up in Ian's dining room, the light streaming in through the giant windows.

"Thattagirl. I guess my job here is done. But I don't mind telling you I'm crazed with jealousy. It's like you walked through a mirror into some kind of fantasy."

"Yeah, I guess I kind of did." She shook her head and smiled to herself. It was pretty surreal. "Thanks for talking me down from the ledge."

"We should all have such a ledge."

"Go back to sleep," Nina said, laughing. "I'll call you soon."

"You do that, sweetie."

Nina hung up, still grinning. Thank God for Stacy.

She stood up and stretched her arms high above her head, feeling light and free of care.

Time for some shopping.

Chapter Six

A few hours later she arrived back at the apartment, laden with bags and shivering with delight. At first she just sat in the middle of Ian's bed and looked at all her goodies, imagining what she'd be able to do with them. She was dying to start painting, but since she didn't know where he wanted her to work, she made do stretching canvases and organizing her supplies the rest of the afternoon.

She was daydreaming about what she'd start on first when she heard a key in the front door. Keeping herself to a respectable walk she got to Ian just as he was putting down his briefcase. God he looked good. She'd never gone for the suit and tie type before, but he wore them with such ease and confidence.

"Honey, I'm home," he announced, grinning mischievously at her. "How was your day?"

"Fantastic, thanks to you," she said, running her hands under his coat as she stood on her toes to kiss him. Instantly his arms were around her, his mouth slanting over hers.

"I thought about you all day," he said, his voice raspy with need.

His hands dove into her hair and his body pressed against hers until she felt every hard-worked muscle, felt his cock throbbing against her and knew how hard and hot it would be. God bless his athlete's body, up for anything and always ready.

Dropping to her knees she grabbed hold of his belt and quickly unbuckled it.

"Holy shit, Nina," he said, falling back against the door and groaning as she unbuttoned and unzipped, releasing his hard length into her hand. She'd never gotten on her knees for a man, but with him it felt both naughty and completely natural.

Her mouth closed over him, sucking him in and out, licking along the seam to the sensitive end where she lingered, letting her tongue and lips torment him.

His breath came harsh and fast until he was invoking both her and the lord mindlessly. He was close, his hips moving, his hands clenched in her hair. She took him deep, her hand tight on his shaft, reveling in how his powerful body responded to her slightest touch. Her own heart beat faster, as if she, too, were close to peaking.

"I'm coming, baby," he said, perhaps to warn her, to give her time to pull away.

But she wasn't going anywhere. Though she'd never been one to swallow, she wanted to take Ian to the end. So she drank him in as he came, his hands fisted in her hair as he let loose with a long, full-throated groan of release.

She sat back on her heels, loving the way he looked at her, like she was the sexiest woman on earth. His eyes were heavy-lidded, his cheeks flushed. He pulled her up, his hands going to her hips to pull her in for a kiss.

"What did I do to deserve that little treat?" he asked. Still leaning against the door, he let his eyes drift shut, though a little smile remained.

"I guess I was just inspired. All kinds of ideas are whirling around in my head ever since I got my supplies."

His eyes opened. "I was worried you might take it the wrong way, but I hated the thought that you wouldn't be able to paint while you were here." A teasing glint in his eye replaced the seriousness. "Had I known there'd be a life-altering bj in the bargain, I wouldn't have hesitated."

Nina laughed, pleased and embarrassed, her face flushing under his warm gaze.

"You don't mind if I temporarily set up a studio in the dining room, do you?" she asked. "I'd really love to get started tomorrow."

"Like I'd refuse you anything now. Let's have dinner and then I'll help you. How about tonight we order in."

"Deal."

They ordered Indian food from the place on the corner and ate it on the sofa, the supplies Nina had bought spread out around them. Afterwards they rearranged his dining room, pushing aside the table and chairs to make room for her easel, spreading a tarp on the floor.

Ian surveyed the room as if looking for other things to heft or wrangle. "Maybe we should get one of those rolling cart things with drawers, so you can store everything and still have easy access."

"That seems like overkill for just a couple of weeks, don't you think?"

Ian frowned at the floor.

"The light in here is amazing," she said, not wanting to think about what happened in two weeks. "I can't wait to get started tomorrow."

***

For the next week, Nina got up every morning with Ian and painted straight through until he came home, stopping only to eat and bathe. She was so caught up in what she was doing, she neglected to check her email for several days. Tuesday morning came around and she opened it up while drinking her coffee, quickly scanning for anything important.

In her inbox was an email from Angela Carter, a fellow student from The Art Institute. Angela had been a year ahead of her in the program and they hadn't known each other especially well, so Nina hadn't emailed her directly about needing a job. Angela was still in Chicago, working for an advertising agency. The email had been sent Monday morning.

Hi Nina, I heard from Craig Miller about your job search, and I may have something for you. My company is looking to hire an entry-level illustrator, so I showed them that series you did a few years back for Charlotte's line of clothing. They said you were just what they were looking for. Unfortunately, we're already in the middle of interviews here, so you'd have to come out immediately to be considered. You can crash at my place for a few nights. Of course, you'd have to sell out like me, so if you're not into it I totally understand. The pay's just about enough to live on and you get decent benefits. It's not a bad company, for what it is. Let me know what you think. Would love to have you out here!

Nina stared at the screen, her mind whirling. Everything in her rebelled at the idea of moving so far away from New York.

From Ian.

If only she had more time to consider. Though she and Ian hardly ever broached the topic, the plan had been to stay until at least this coming weekend, maybe even a little longer. Just the other day he'd told her she should stay until she found something worthwhile, as if he were in no hurry for her to leave. But she couldn't stay here forever. Ian had a life, and she needed to get one too.

Her heart sank at the thought of having to squeeze her painting time in on evenings and weekends. That would hurt, but she couldn't afford to be fussy. She was lucky to get a chance at a job like this. She'd applied for similar positions in New York this past year, but with so many people applying for every opening, most of them with at least some advertising experience, she hadn't even gotten an interview.

Ignoring the pit in her stomach, she did a search on flights and booked one leaving that day at noon, returning Friday. That way if they wanted to see her a second day, or she needed to look for an apartment, she could do it all in one trip. It was money she couldn't afford to spend unless it led to more money, so something needed to come of it.

She wrote Angela back and told her she'd be there by early afternoon, and Angela replied with instructions to call when she landed.

Now all she had to do was tell Ian.

She called his cell and left a message when he didn't answer. There was no telling when he'd be free to check his voicemail, as he had a slew of important meetings that day.

Would he be upset when he heard, or happy for her?

She was getting ahead of herself. There was no guarantee they'd hire her. Even if they did, they might not make a decision for weeks. Either way, it wasn't like she'd never see Ian again.

She jumped in the shower, then quickly printed a couple copies of her résumé, packed her two good suits and grabbed her portfolio. Jittery with anxiety and too much coffee, she looked around the apartment one last time.

Why did she feel as if she were leaving for good? Or worse, running out on Ian?

Going back into the bedroom, she pulled out her lacy black underwear and laid it on the bed along with a post-it note saying she would see him soon. Then she kissed it, her lipsticked mouth leaving a deep red imprint.

That was more like it. Best to leave him something light-hearted and sexy, conveying the fact that she'd be back in no time and they could pick up where they'd left off.

For a little while, at least.

***

Desperate for some air after the marathon negotiations, Ian pushed open the doors to his building and stepped outside, blinking in the bright sun. Crossing the street to the Starbucks on the corner he stood in line for a coffee, mulling over what he and Nina should do for dinner. Looking at his watch, he realized he hadn't called her yet today. Normally he checked in by noon and it was already after one. Pulling out his phone he smiled when he saw she'd already called him.

God, he loved her sweet, husky voice. Every time he heard it, whether in person or over the phone, a little thrill went through him at the sound. It was immature, but he couldn't wait to tell her how the negotiations had gone, how he'd held firm and played super-lawyer until the other counsel backed down. It was a ridiculous ego trip, but he loved impressing her. If he could have killed a mastodon and dragged it to her feet, he'd have done that too.

Then he listened to her message and all the pleasure went out of the day.

He hung up the phone and immediately tried to call her, but there was no answer. She was probably still in the air. Damn it.

Why was everyone taking so long to order a friggin' cup of coffee? You'd think people would have the options figured out by now, but no, they stood there debating whether or not to get the gingerbread latte or peppermint mocha, as if they were the only people in line.

"Tall French roast," he ordered when he finally made it to the counter. Or maybe he kind of snarled it, because the skinny kid behind the counter flinched and his hand shook as he handed him his change. Christ. He was acting like an asshole. He needed to get a grip.

As soon as his coffee came he grabbed it and launched himself back outside, grateful for the biting wind.

So fine, Nina was interviewing for a job in Chicago. It was unexpected, but he'd known she'd be leaving soon. Anyway, she had to come back. All her stuff was in New York, most of it at his place. It wasn't like he'd never see her again. Maybe she wouldn't even get the job. You could never tell what employers were looking for.

Guilt flooded him at this pathetic hope. He should want what was best for Nina, regardless of how it affected him. Of course, her painting would have to take a back seat if she was working full time at an ad agency, but that was her call.

His buzz over the day's meetings was gone, and he couldn't shake the moroseness that had descended. Tempted as he was to keep calling her, he made himself wait. He'd left her a message, and she'd get back to him when she could.

Jesus, what kind of a wuss was he that he couldn't handle three days without her?

His bad mood stuck around the rest of the afternoon, and didn't improve when he entered his empty apartment, its silence broadcasting Nina's absence. Never once in all the years he'd lived here, even after Karen had moved out, had he felt lonely coming home. Until now.

Desperate to shed his suit, he was already loosening his tie as he stalked into his bedroom.

A pair of her sexy black underwear lay in the center of the quilt, a playful little note beside it. He'd pulled the same scrap of lace off her a few days ago. With perfect clarity he recalled the little sounds she'd made, not to mention the things she'd done to him with that hot, sweet mouth.

Instantly he was hard, his raging erection totally useless and unwanted. Welcome to the next three days.

Within minutes he was in his workout clothes and heading over to the gym, where he set himself a grueling series of core exercises followed by his second run of the day. The punishing workout left him somewhat calmer, though it didn't stop him from wondering how Nina was making out in Chicago. He checked his cell once he got home. No messages.

Pulling out leftovers from the last few days he nuked them in the microwave, then ate listlessly in front of the TV like the bachelor he was. Nina called midway through *The Outlaw Josey Wales*, his favorite Clint Eastwood flick, though even Clint hadn't managed to raise his spirits tonight. He muted the TV but made himself wait two rings before answering.

"Nina."

"Hi, Ian."

There it was, that tantalizing voice of hers. But tonight he heard a hint of uncertainty, and he knew her well enough by now that he could picture her biting her lip as she waited for him to speak.

"How are things in Chicago?"

"Oh, fine. I'm sorry about leaving like I did, though."

"Don't worry about it. It's not your fault I couldn't get to the phone. Are you interviewing tomorrow?"

"I met some of the managers this afternoon, but my formal interview is tomorrow morning. They seemed to like me, I guess. I don't know. The department's not as creative as I was hoping, and the work would be pretty boring," she said, sounding forlorn. "But I suppose it's a good opportunity."

Ian didn't reply immediately. He wanted to wish her luck and give her encouragement, but his brain revolted at the idea of her working there. As a result, nothing came out of his mouth.

"Ian?"

"Just take it one step at a time," he counseled. Jesus, he sounded like his father.

"Yeah, I guess that's what I'll do."

There was an excited babble of voices in the background and then she spoke again. "I'd better run. Angela is having me meet a couple of friends who need a new housemate, and they just arrived."

"Sure, no problem. Good luck tomorrow. Call me after your interview and let me know how it went."

"Of course. Bye, Ian."

Ian sat there with the phone still in his hand for several minutes, trying to figure out why he felt so terrible. Part of it was how bummed out she sounded, like she was going to take the job because she thought she had no choice.

Should he have said something else, told her not to take it if she didn't want it? He didn't want her to go, especially if she wasn't going to be happy, but they'd known all along this was going to happen.

He went to bed soon afterwards and dreamed of Nina, though in the morning he remembered nothing but the feeling of having lost her.

Nina finally called at eleven the next morning.

"They offered me the job," she said, her voice flat.

"Wow, that was fast."

"I know," she said, with what sounded like resignation. "They liked my work, and they need people in there as soon as possible."

"Did you give them an answer yet?"

"Not officially. They have to put together a formal offer with benefits and everything. Human resources will get in touch in the next few days."

"Right. That makes sense." He paused. "You don't sound too thrilled," he ventured.

"Thrilled isn't the word I'd use, but it'll be fine. I know I'm lucky to have this. It just hasn't quite sunk in yet, I guess."

She spoke without any of her usual enthusiasm or wry humor. It was almost like he was talking to a different person.

"Are you still coming home – I mean back – on Friday?"

"Yes. My plane lands at four o'clock."

"I have a meeting at three-thirty so I don't think I can get away then, but I'll have the car pick you up and try to get home right afterwards."

"You don't need to order the car. I can get back just fine."

"Don't bother trying to talk me out of it. It's a done deal."

"Okay, okay," she said, as if he were overdoing it, but he would have bet anything she was secretly pleased.

They talked for another minute before hanging up. Just two more days to get through before seeing her. Then she would leave, and he'd have too many days to count.

***

Nina paused outside Ian's apartment door, her heart beating like mad. Until now she'd always walked right in, but this time she was hesitant, as if she no longer had the right. The worst part was, his apartment felt like home. She couldn't remember the last time she'd felt so good somewhere, so welcome. Not even her own parents had managed to give her that.

And now she had to leave it.

Knocking lightly, she waited, the sound of a Tom Waits ballad drifting through the door. Her heart squeezed as she remembered the time they'd made love to that very song.

She must have knocked too softly, because he didn't open the door. This was getting ridiculous. Testing the doorknob she found it already open, so she let herself in, stepping inside and dropping her bags.

"Hello?" she called out.

Then Ian was coming down the hallway from his bedroom, dressed in a worn pair of jeans and a sweatshirt. God, he looked good.

"Hey," he said, stopping a few feet away, his hands shoved in his pockets as he smiled uncertainly at her.

Not quite the welcome she'd expected.

"Hey, yourself," she said. Walking over to him she wrapped her arms around his waist, closing her eyes as she absorbed the feel of him. He stayed tense for a few moments before gradually relaxing on a long breath.

"It's good to see you, baby," he said, his arms coming around her at last.

"It's good to be back," she murmured, her heart aching at the thought of having to let him go.

Then her stomach growled in an embarrassingly obvious plea for sustenance. Ian pulled away.

"You must be hungry. Let's go get a bite and you can tell me everything while we eat."

They headed to a favorite Italian place around the corner and Ian asked all about her trip – what her co-workers were like, what kinds of campaigns she'd be working on, how it was to be back in Chicago again.

She answered his questions without elaborating, not all that keen on talking about a job she didn't really want. She didn't add how much she was going to miss him, or how hard she was working to convince herself she was happy. Her presence in his home had always hinged on the fact that she would get a job and leave. No way was she going to make it sound like that was a problem now. They were grown-ups and they had an understanding. It was her problem if she was having a hard time now that the day had finally come.

And who knew? Maybe they'd still see each other from time to time. There was no shortage of flights between New York and Chicago.

"I'm sure it'll be great," he said, sounding as unconvincing as she did.

Was it possible he was going to miss her too?

They were both quiet when they got back to the apartment. Nina busied herself in the bedroom unpacking her bags, her stomach in knots at the thought of how soon she'd be repacking them. She was folding her clothes on the bed when Ian came in.

"I missed you," he said, wrapping his arms around her from behind and nuzzling her neck. But instead of his usual playfulness he sounded somber, already mournful.

Turning around in his arms, she ran her hands up his back to the nape of his neck, tugging him down for a kiss. Their lips met, his tongue slipping inside her mouth as he groaned low in his throat. It felt like forever since she'd last tasted him.

Then he was easing her back onto the bed as he followed her down. Their bodies fused together and she ran her hands under his sweatshirt, her fingers tracing the play of muscles under warm skin. She kissed him with increasing fervor, rubbed her cheek along the slight stubble of his jaw.

There was so much to feel, to memorize, before she left.

Ian pulled away and looked down at her, his fingers brushing her hair back from her forehead. Her throat tightened at the intensity of his gaze and a spear of longing for something else – something more – slid through her, taking her breath.

Her throat clogged and she felt the sting of tears before she knew what was happening.

Ian frowned down at her with concern.

"What's wrong, baby?"

Nina sniffled, trying to get a grip, and managed a wobbly smile. "I was just thinking about how strange it'll be to leave here. Just ignore me."

For a moment he didn't say anything, and she started to panic. Had she been too revealing?

"You don't have to leave," he finally replied.

Nina froze, not sure if she understood him correctly. "Of course I do. That was the deal."

"We could change the deal. You could live here with me."

She sat up and stared at him, dumbfounded.

"But we barely know each other."

"I don't know about that. Anyway, what I do know of you I'm crazy about. It makes no sense for you to leave, not when things are so great with us."

"But there are no jobs around here," she protested. "Trust me, I've been looking."

"Forget that. You've worked hard enough. Let me take care of you."

"That's crazy," she said, shaking her head. "No way would I just freeload off you."

"I have more than enough for both of us. Let me make things easier for you. There's no harm in that, is there? Think of it this way. Your job will be to paint. The ad agency can find another illustrator, but no one else can paint the way you do."

"I don't know," she said, holding her spinning head in her hands. She could hardly conceive of all her daily burdens being lifted, just like that, by Ian. But it wasn't that simple. "What if I give up this job and then in a few weeks or months we decide it's not working?"

"It's a risk, I'm not saying it isn't. There's no guarantee we'll live happily ever after, but I sure as hell want to try." He took her hand in his and looked at her, his gaze locked on hers. "I love you, Nina. I can't stand the thought of you leaving now."

She'd never allowed herself to want those words from him, hadn't allowed herself to even think about loving him. But as soon as he said them, the truth welled up in her, and there was no holding back her own feelings.

Her heart raced at the risk she was about to take. And not just with him but with herself. What if, even with all the time and resources in the world to devote to her painting, she still didn't have what it took? There'd be no excuses, no hiding from the truth then.

But that was the chance she had to take, because there was no way she was leaving now. The most incredible man she'd ever known was offering her everything she could want, her own personal heaven. She had only to accept it.

All at once the sadness and worry she'd been carrying disappeared, as if a shade had been lifted in a dark room, dazzling her with light.

"I love you, too," she said, smiling shyly, the feelings between them so new they left her with a kind of disbelieving joy.

She couldn't stop the tears from welling up, but they were good ones, born out of all the love and hope surging through her, overflowing the confines of her body.

"Thank God," he said, smiling into her eyes.

He kissed her then, a slow, melting kiss full of heat and tenderness. They were both good and breathless when he pulled back and looked at her.

"Welcome home, Nina."

Want more of Ian and Nina? Read the rest of their story in *Keep Me:*

What started off as a fling with Ian Sinclair is now a full-on love affair, and Nina Valentine can hardly believe her good fortune. Life with Ian gets more delicious every day, and after years of struggle all she has to worry about is her art.

But it's not long before her doubts resurface and she's once again wondering if she fits in Ian's world. As generous as he is, she hates taking his money, and everyone from her own mother to Ian's friends seems to think less of her for it.

Alone in their little love nest the two of them make sense, but as soon as they let the outside world in, it all starts to fall apart. People are starting to talk, and she doesn't like what they're saying. Even worse, she's starting to believe them.

About the Author

Isabel began reading romances at the age of fourteen. That's the year her grandmother came to visit, bringing with her a shopping bag filled with (very tame) Harlequin and Silhouette romance novels. Isabel was immediately and forever hooked. What could be better than experiencing all that lust and new love just by reading a book?

Sign up for Isabel's newsletter at www.isabelmorin.com and get new release alerts and exclusive content. Your email address will never be shared, and you can unsubscribe at any time.

Email Isabel at isabel@isabelmorin.com. She'd love to hear from you!

Liked the book? Consider leaving a review!